MURDER OF A GENTLEMAN

Gripping fiction by a great storyteller

PIPPA McCATHIE

THE
BOOK
FOLKS

Paperback published by The Book Folks

London, 2022

ISBN 978-1-80462-032-8

www.thebookfolks.com

*This book is dedicated to Julia
and all those who work at the Wessex Cancer Trust.*

Prologue

It was the howling of the dogs that first attracted his attention on that bleak Friday morning in April. It was as he parked his motorbike and took off his helmet that he first heard them, but he couldn't see them. He looked around. Where the hell were they? The house loomed before him, built of imposing grey granite for some Victorian magnate. It was tucked away on the road from Pontygwyn to Abergavenny and overshadowed by tall, imposing pines to one side, bending slightly away from the prevailing wind. It was if they were protecting it.

The howling continued. He thought he could tell now where the two Dobermanns were. It was definitely both Chester and Jasper. He made his way quickly round, his boots crunching on the gravel as he ran. An ancient apple tree stood a few feet from the house, its topmost branches almost touching a narrow balcony with ceiling-to-floor windows behind it. The windows were wide open. At the base of the tree he noticed what looked like a pile of clothes crumpled up below its branches. But a hand, palm up, protruded from them. A foot away the dogs stood side by side, their heads lifted as they howled their distress.

He rushed over, heart beating fast, and they both looked round at him. The howling stopped. "Okay, boys. Chester, Jasper, it's okay, it's okay," he soothed as he approached them. He knew them both well, but it would be sensible to be wary of them when they were in such a state.

Neither of them moved, nor did they start their howling again. They watched, dark brown eyes pleading. He bent down by what he now knew was a body. He recognised the jacket, and the black and white shemagh scarf round the neck. The body was lying on its side, one arm awkwardly twisted and outflung, the other underneath. On the back of the head was a large, indented wound.

"Are you alright, sir?" he said. Stupid, of course he wasn't. There was no movement, not a stir except from the dogs who'd come up close behind him, watching and wary.

He thought back to that first aid course he'd done and remembered where to feel for a pulse. Pulling off his driving gloves, he picked up the flaccid wrist and, as he did so, noticed a large sprig of rosemary clasped in the fingers. Strange, there was no rosemary in this part of the garden. When he drew his hand away, he saw that it was stained with blood.

"Shit, shit, shit." He bent closer. The eyes were half open, but there was no sign of life.

He looked up at the window guarded by the decorative wrought iron. Did he fall from there? he wondered. If he had, surely he would have been lying, well, more untidily. But there was no point in speculating. What should he do? Go into the house? But no. There'd been no small white Fiat on the gravel. She must be out.

What would I do now if I was actually in the police? he wondered. He'd been thinking of applying to join the Gwent force. But this was wasting time.

He took his mobile from the back pocket of his jeans and pressed in the three digits.

Chapter 1

"What do you mean, you can't come?" Fabia Havard exclaimed, glaring at her partner Matt Lambert's reflection in the bathroom mirror. She turned to face him, her toothbrush held like a weapon in her hand.

Matt stood in the doorway and ran a hand through his dark hair, making it look even more untidy than it usually did. "I'm sorry, really sorry, but it's a three-line whip. I got a text from Dilys while you were in the shower. The new chief's calling a meeting of all the staff while it's supposedly quiet at the station. Everyone's got to be on parade."

"And that's more important than the antenatal class?"

"No – yes – no. Fabia darling, you should know what it's like. You've been there, done that."

"But I haven't given birth before," Fabia snapped, pushing aside his reasonable comment. She wasn't in any mood to be reasonable. "This class is important, Matt. Apart from anything else, I think it's when they tell you what to expect when I'm in labour."

"I know, I know. But I'm afraid it can't be helped."

He moved towards her, but she pushed past him into the bedroom, sat down at the dressing table and began to pull a hairbrush through her curly hair.

She felt his warm hand on her shoulder. "Look, I'm really sorry, darling, but I have to go. You can tell me all about it when I get home, and I'm sure they'll be able to tell you where I can do a pile of research, YouTube videos and all that."

"That's not the same, though, is it?" Fabia complained, unable to get out of this self-pitying groove she seemed to be stuck in. "Okay, go. Go. I'll see you later."

He bent to kiss her, but she turned her head so that the kiss landed on her cheek. Matt stood still for a moment frowning at her, then shrugged, grabbed his jacket and bounded downstairs and out of the front door. It banged shut behind him.

Fabia dropped her head in her hands. "Damn, damn, damn," she said. Matt was right, she did know what it was like. For goodness sake, it was only four years ago that she'd retired from the Gwent force, a superintendent herself then. The arrival of a new chief always concentrated minds and loomed large. Matt, as the local chief inspector, would be very much on parade, as he'd put it, as would the rest of his team.

Since his previous boss's retirement, which had been a relief to all concerned, including Fabia, they looked forward to the arrival of his replacement. When Matt first met Chief Superintendent Erica Talbot he'd told Fabia he'd found it hard to suss her out. He'd said she was very cool and controlled and described her as closed-in. She was coming in from the Derbyshire force and he'd been worried she might not be up to scratch on South Wales and its idiosyncrasies, but he'd said it was obvious she'd done her homework. Later he'd found out her family came from Cwmbran, not that far from Pontygwyn.

But still, Fabia thought, this pregnancy is a first for both of us. She rubbed at her bulging middle as she felt the baby kick. Surely, Matt could have explained. Shouldn't it be easier to get through to a woman about this kind of thing? No, said her more reasonable self. But still– Her thoughts were interrupted by her mobile phone. She picked it up from the bedside table and, glancing at the screen, she sighed with relief. She swiped at the arrow and said, "Thank goodness it's only you?"

"Only me, thanks a bunch," said her close friend, Cath Temple, vicar of St Cybi's church.

"Sorry," Fabia said. "It's just that I'm in a foul mood. At least I don't have to pretend with you, love."

"Oh dear. What's up?"

"Matt's new boss, Erica Talbot – you know, I told you about her? She's called a meeting of all staff which he says he can't miss." Fabia gave a gusty sigh. "Trouble is he should be coming with me to my antenatal class this morning, it's the one where they go through what labour entails and what Matt should expect."

"And he's gone off to meet his new boss?"

"Exactly. He said it was a three-line whip."

"Well, it would be, I suppose."

"I know, but still."

"I'm sure there's plenty of research he can do online, Fabia. You told me he's pretty keen to know exactly what goes on."

"That's what he said. It's just that I'm a bit scared and wanted him there to hold my hand."

"Scared of what?"

Fabia chewed at her bottom lip for a moment, then burst out, "Of finding out what happens." She could hear Cath give a muffled snort and protested, "What are you laughing at?"

"Oh, Fabia, you are such a strange mixture. Ex-senior police officer, promoted way beyond what most women achieve in the police force, and now you're a talented, sought-after artist, a career change that very few people could manage, and here you are getting yourself into a stew about something that squillions of women do all over the world. Anyway, you've done plenty of reading and stuff, haven't you?"

Fabia chose not to answer this question. "That doesn't mean it isn't bloody scary, particularly at my age," she protested.

When she'd found out she was expecting it had come as a shock to Fabia. She and Matt had never been particularly careful about contraception, thinking that at forty-two she was hardly likely to get pregnant, but a few months ago, after several weeks of feeling queasy and exhausted, Fabia had done the test. Matt's delight at the news had surprised her and, once she'd persuaded him that he didn't have to treat her as if she was an invalid, they'd got on with their life.

"I've assisted in many a birth, Fabia," Cath said, who'd been a nurse before she was ordained. "You'll be fine, pet. Look, where is the class?"

"At the medical centre in Usk."

"What time?"

"Ten thirty."

"Okay, so why don't you pop into the vicarage afterwards and tell me all about it, I can give you some lunch, after all it is meant to be my day off."

"That'd be great," Fabia said. "I seem to be permanently hungry these days, so you'd better get in extra supplies."

Cath laughed. "Will do," she said, "I'll see you later."

* * *

Matt swore quietly to himself. Being held up on the M4 was just what he needed this morning. He glanced at the dashboard clock – twenty to nine. The meeting with the chief superintendent was scheduled for nine o'clock and he'd wanted to spend time getting some notes together beforehand. At this rate, if the traffic didn't clear, he'd be lucky if he made it in time for the meeting itself, let alone in time to do any preparation. He called his sergeant, Dilys Bevan, on the hands-free.

"I'm snarled up in traffic, Dilys, probably an accident up ahead. I might be late. Can you make my excuses?"

"No problem, sir, will do." As always, Dilys was calm and unflustered.

But only a few minutes later she was calling him back. She sounded worried.

"Sir, we've had a call in from a PC Emrys Barton. He answered a 999 call up to Carreg Llwyd House, says the gardener, Craig Evans, found a body in the grounds."

Matt went cold. "Has it been identified?" he snapped.

"I'm afraid so, sir. It's Geraint Denbigh and it looks as if he fell from a window on the first floor. He's dead and Barton and the medics that were called aren't happy with what they found. It seems Craig Evans told them they should contact you as you're a friend of his, or Fabia is."

"More Fabia than me," Matt said. "Oh shit, this is going to be a nightmare on so many different fronts. Have you told the chief super?"

"Not yet."

"Right," Matt said. "Hang on till I get in. I'm nearly there."

Matt swore colourfully. Geraint Denbigh. That was a name to conjure with. He was to Pontygwyn what Anthony Hopkins was to Port Talbot.

Fabia had been rummaging around in the attic a few weeks ago and she'd found a wooden box, about the size of a large shoe box, tucked behind the cradle she'd been looking for. There had been a roughly carved love spoon stuck to the top and inside were loads of letters. All but one had been from the writer and film director, Geraint Denbigh, to Fabia's Auntie Meg. And there had been photos too; some just of him, some of the two of them together. He was unmistakable, that face like a benevolent satyr, the jutting nose and hooded eyes. Her aunt had written on the back of some of the photos, things like

'Darling Geraint and me at Barry Island, April 1963' and another said, 'Walking along the Brecon canal two days before Geraint left for London'. That had been dated June 1963.

Fabia had taken the box to Geraint. She said he should have them. At first he'd been wary, thinking that she wanted something from him, or that she'd kept some back to sell to the tabloids. But once she'd convinced him that she had no such intention, they'd become firm friends. He'd apologised for doubting her and told her about the autobiography he was writing.

"I had a stroke a few years back," he'd said. "It was one of the reasons I came home to Wales, for some peace and quiet while I write my autobiography. And that, my dear, is going to open up a hell of a can of worms! It's going to make the #MeToo campaign look like a walk in the park for some. But I can tell you one person who'll come out of my story with nothing but praise – and regret for what I did – and that's your lovely Aunt Meggie."

Apparently, they'd been childhood sweethearts and had planned to marry. But Geraint's father had chucked him out and he'd made his way to London to find work. He'd told Meggie he'd be sending for her when he'd got a job and somewhere to live, but she hadn't been able to go. She'd had too many family commitments back in Pontygwyn.

More recently Geraint had asked to speak to Matt. Recently he'd been plagued by unpleasant e-mails and phone calls. All had mentioned the autobiography that he was writing and threatened retribution if he published. Geraint had put it all down to the plague of the paparazzi, but Matt had his doubts.

And now Geraint was dead. How on earth were they going to keep the lid on that? Geraint's high profile would have the paparazzi buzzing round like hornets. He must warn his team to keep things to themselves, even more than they usually did.

Matt swore again and drummed an irritated tattoo on the steering wheel as he negotiated the roundabouts that led into the centre of Newport. He drove on past the Steel Wave, an enormous red circular sculpture which commemorated the importance of the steel industry to the area, and past a newer addition to the banks of the river Usk, an elegant new footbridge which spanned the river. He saw none of it. He was too busy wondering what on earth had happened. He had a bad feeling about this. But speculation was pointless. That didn't stop him turning it over and over in his mind.

Chapter 2

Later that morning Geraint's sister, Glenda Armitage, and her daughter, Mari Reynolds, were being shown to a table in a small restaurant in the Royal Arcade in Cardiff.

Glenda was a small, thin woman, who looked as if a gust of wind could blow her away. A slight stoop gave her a bird-like air, but she was immaculately dressed as usual, her grey hair glossy and rigidly styled, her make-up perfect. She straightened her Hobbs jacket and carefully placed her Burberry handbag by her feet. Mari watched her as she did so and wished she could afford clothes as expensive as her mother's. Not going to happen, though, is it, she thought resentfully.

"Why did you choose this place?" Glenda asked, looking round the room at the bare wood floor, the scrubbed oak tables and mixture of chairs. "It's a bit rough and ready isn't it?"

"No, Mother, it's one of the most popular vegetarian restaurants in Cardiff."

"Vegetarian? Ah," Glenda said with the lift of a mocking eyebrow, "still on that kick, are you?"

"Yup, still caring about animals and the way they're slaughtered," Mari said, knowing she was rising to the bait.

"Bless you, darling, you always have been a softy." From Glenda, this didn't sound like a compliment.

"That's me," Mari said, giving her mother a defiant smile. "Shall we have a look at the menu? Their food is delicious."

Yet again that mocking eyebrow was raised but there was no further comment as her mother bent to take a pair of slim glasses from her handbag and put them on. For a moment there was silence as they read through the menus. A waitress came up to them, asked what they'd like to drink and if they were ready to order.

"Mineral water for me," Glenda said. "I don't suppose you have any Ty Nant spring water?" She looked slightly put out when the waitress said they did.

"Same for me," said Mari, wishing she had the courage to order a large glass of wine. She felt she needed it.

They ordered their food. Mari chose the butternut risotto and, after a lot of umming and ahhing, and questions put to the patient waitress, her mother chose spinach and ricotta lasagne. "At least the lasagne bit is familiar," she said to Mari with a tight smile.

When the waitress had left them, Glenda lent back in her chair and looked across at her daughter. "So how is work going?" she asked.

"It's really great, insanely busy. We've got a new project that we're hoping will be picked up by Channel 4 which is very exciting."

"What kind of project?"

"It's a black comedy about the film world, spanning both the UK and the US, so we're hoping it'll be popular on both sides of the Atlantic."

"It sounds like the kind of thing your uncle would be involved in."

"Oh no, it was Tenniel's idea, bless him, and it's really taken off," Mari assured her. "It would be fantastic if one of the American streamers got involved."

"Streamers?" her mother asked, eyebrows raised.

"Networks, TV streamers. But we mustn't get our hopes up. Channel 4 will do fine for now." Mari paused, wondering how to say what was in her mind. In the end, she just took the plunge. "I'm going to ask Uncle Geraint for advice on the US side."

"Why on earth would you do that?" her mother demanded.

Mari sighed, then said patiently, "Because he's very well known in the business, he's worked in both countries, and he might have some pointers. You said yourself it sounded like something he'd be interested in."

"Granted, but I wouldn't go anywhere near him if I were you," Glenda said. "He'll just tell you to get on with it and leave him alone, or he'll steal the idea from you."

"No, he won't, he's not got anything on the go at the moment," Mari said defensively. "I've seen quite a bit of him lately, ever since he came back to Wales, in fact. He was working on an idea for a TV series back then, but I think he might have given up on that. Anyway, we get on. I've always liked him, even if he is a bit chopsy."

"What's that mean?"

"Argumentative, stroppy."

"That's putting it mildly," Glenda snapped. "More like deceitful, disagreeable, selfish… I could go on."

"I'd much rather you didn't," Mari said quietly. "I wish the two of you…" She paused, wondering whether to continue.

"What do you wish?"

"I wish you two got on," she said in a rush, "especially now he's had the stroke and isn't so well."

"He's tough as old boots, your uncle," Glenda said dismissively. "Bound to see us all out."

Before Mari could stop herself, she asked, "What was it that went so wrong? What did he do to make you, well, hate him so?"

"I don't hate him," Glenda snapped. "And I don't want to talk about it. How is Tenniel? Have you two got together at last?"

This too was shaky ground and Mari was relieved when they were interrupted by the waitress with their food. By the time she'd left them to their meal, the atmosphere had calmed a little. Mari decided to change the subject, get on to safer ground, so she asked, "How long are you staying at Annedd Wen this time?"

Annedd Wen, her parent's house just outside Caerleon, was so called because it was an old farmhouse that had always been painted white. It stood on a hill just to the east of the old Roman town. It was one of three homes they owned. Her stepfather, Jonathan, lived most of the time in a flat in a Georgian house in Islington. He was a hedge fund manager who'd also dabbled in property development; he did not lack for money, that was for sure. They also lived some of the year at a house they owned in Tuscany, but her mother spent more time in Wales.

"I'm not sure," Glenda said, in answer to Mari's question. "I've got to supervise the decorators. They can't be trusted to do everything as I want it. They're starting on the lounge and dining room at the end of the week. Although I have to go up to London to look at curtain materials and suchlike, I'll probably be here for a few weeks at least. But never mind about me, you haven't told me about Tenniel."

"We're not an item, Mam, just friends who work together, that's all it's ever been."

Tenniel Darling and Mari had met at university where they'd been close but platonic friends. Like her, he too was from South Wales. His parents, both dead now, had been teachers from Swansea. There had been a time when she'd thought she and Tenniel might be more than just close friends, but it had never seemed right and gradually she'd realised her interests lay in another direction. He'd gone on to have a series of girlfriends, each one more glamorous than the last, and Mari had fallen for one of her female lecturers.

That relationship hadn't ended well and Tenniel, with casual kindness, had been there to pick up the pieces and help her back on her feet. She'd always been grateful to him for that and, when a few years later he'd asked her to help him set up Cariad Productions, so called because of Tenniel's surname, she'd been happy to put money into it, mainly from a trust fund set up for her by her father. Her uncle had put a small amount of money into the company as well, but only on condition she didn't tell her mother.

The move back to Wales and opening an office in Cardiff Bay had seemed like a no-brainer since the popularity of Cardiff as a hub for production companies and the Dr Who phenomenon had blossomed. Now Cariad Productions was beginning to make its mark with Tenniel as CEO and founder, and Mari as a fellow founder and creative director, although Tenniel often told Mari she was too naïve for this business. "You're such a softy," he'd say. "So – sort of – moral." Then he'd follow it up with, "But your imagination is second to none." He'd smile and hug her, and she'd forget about the criticism.

"Come on, darling," her mother said now. "You two were very close at university. I always thought you would end up together, after all, it was obvious to me that you were more than just colleagues."

"It may have seemed so to you, Mother, but it's not going to happen." Mari took a deep breath. She'd always known a time would come when she'd have to tell her mother that she wasn't interested in men, and now that she was in a serious relationship, there was no escaping telling her the truth.

"Why not?" her mother demanded.

"Because– because that's not the way TD and I feel about each other, and anyway, I've met someone else."

Her mother's eyes widened, and she asked eagerly, "Who is he?"

Taking a deep breath, Mari said, "Not he, she."

Glenda stared across the table at her daughter, a fork full of lasagne suspended halfway to her open mouth. She put the food slowly back on to her plate. "Are you telling me," she said, dropping her voice almost to a whisper, "that you're a *lesbian*?" Given her tone, she might as well have been asking if Mari was a drug pusher.

"Yes, I am, and Cassie and I are in love. We're hoping to move in together one of these days," and she added defiantly, "we're hoping to have a baby."

"A baby? How on earth…?"

"Oh, Mother," Mari said wearily. "This is the twenty-first century. Surely you know that same-sex couples can get together, marry, have children nowadays. You know, there are such things as IVF, sperm donors, etc."

A look of distaste came into her mother's face. "Really. That's not the kind of thing I want to talk about over my lunch."

Mari pushed her plate away, no longer interested in the remains of her risotto. She took a gulp of her water then beckoned the waitress and asked her to bring a large glass of the house red. She felt she needed it.

Taking a deep breath, she said, "Cassie is Uncle Geraint's housekeeper, that's how we met."

Her mother glared across at her, her eyes cold, her thin lips tight. "And I suppose he's encouraging this relationship, is he?"

Mari stared across the table at her mother, opened her mouth to respond, then paused as the waitress put her glass of wine down beside her. "Thank you," she said, glancing up at the young woman and smiling. She took a gulp of the wine. "No, he hasn't," she said firmly. "He hasn't really commented, but he certainly hasn't objected to our being close."

"He's probably pushed you into it. It'd be typical of him to use you to get at me."

"What on earth do you mean? That's nonsense."

This decisive response seemed to throw her mother off track. She wasn't used to Mari standing up to her.

"Well" – Glenda straightened the knife and fork on her empty plate then folded her napkin carefully and placed it on the table – "he probably knew I wouldn't exactly be delighted to find out my daughter's chosen to be a– a lesbian, that's why he's been pushing you into the arms of this Cassie woman, to get at me."

"Oh, for fuck's sake!"

"Don't use that disgusting language," her mother said, so tight-lipped Mari was surprised the words could emerge.

She took a deep breath then went on slowly. "First of all, he didn't push me in any way, and he hasn't even mentioned you. Second, it's not a case of choosing, it's what I am, I realise that now."

Thinking a change of subject would take the awkwardness and heat out of the conversation, Mari said, "Did you know Uncle Geraint is writing his autobiography? It's going to be published later this year."

It took seconds for Mari to realise that, subject-wise, she'd gone from the frying pan into the fire.

"He is *what?*" her mother exclaimed, attracting attention from people sitting at nearby tables. After a quick glance either side, she leant forward across the table and, in a furious undertone, said, "What is he going to say? He'll lie, you know. He'll say he didn't desert us and bugger off to London without so much as a by-your-leave."

Mari's eyes widened. She'd never heard her mother use the word 'bugger' before. Talk about hypocrisy! She opened her mouth to respond but wasn't given the chance.

"He'll gloss over leaving me to deal with your grandfather and the disasters that followed, the loss of the land, the loss of our status in the community. No, no" – she waggled a finger in front of Mari – "none of that will be mentioned. Selfish, selfish, that's all he is, that's all he ever was, and I had to pick up the pieces and deal with everything until your grandfather died." Her voice shook slightly, accentuating how upset she was.

Mari finally managed to interrupt the flow. "But, Mam, the land was sold long before he left, and anyway, you had my father to look after you. It's not my uncle's fault that Tadcu drank and sold everything off, Geraint was a teenager then. And he told me he was thrown out and told never to come back."

Her mother gave a snort of derision. "He's done a good job on you. I might have known he'd turn you against me as well. I'm not listening to any more of this." She grabbed up her handbag, rummaged in the depths, brought out a wallet and pulled out some notes. "Here you are, I don't suppose you mind me paying for your lunch?" She slapped the money down on the table and, straightening up, strode out of the restaurant without another word.

Mari sank back in her chair, knowing that other customers were turning curious eyes on her. After a moment she straightened and looked around. Several people pretended they hadn't been staring as she held up a hand to the waitress and, as quickly as she could, downed the rest of her wine, paid the bill and escaped.

Once outside she strode along, dodging other pedestrians, barely aware that they were there. Turning into The Hayes, she walked quickly along towards Cardiff Museum and, a few minutes later, arrived at Cariad Productions. Desperately hoping that everyone else would still be out at lunch, she aimed to head straight for her desk and bury herself in work, but her luck was out. As she walked in, Tenniel came out of his office and headed towards the coffee machine.

Tenniel was a good-looking man in his late thirties, dark-haired and blue-eyed, with a ready smile. He could, when he chose to, be very charming indeed, but Mari knew him too well to be taken in by the charm. She did, however, count him among her closest friends and they worked well together, hence the success of Cariad Productions. It had done well with daytime dramas, but now they felt they were about to hit the big time with *It Could Happen to You*, a satirical look at the very industry her uncle had been part of. Tenniel thought contact with such a luminary of the theatre and film world could do the company nothing but good, although he wasn't sure he wanted Geraint to know too much about the project he'd been working on that morning while Mari was out. There was a negative side to that, one that Mari knew nothing about, and that was how Tenniel wanted it to stay.

"Good, you're back," he said, then added, as if it was an afterthought, "How did the lunch go?"

"Bloody disaster, but that's par for the course with my dear mother," Mari said. "She's definitely not pleased that I've been seeing so much of Uncle Geraint."

"Well, you did say they'd fallen out."

"I know," Mari said wearily. "I just hoped it would be different this time."

"You always say that. I'd say it's a fond hope." He paused. "Did you tell her about the new production?"

"I did. And about Cassie–"

"Uh-oh! What was her reaction to that?"

Mari sighed. "I don't know what made her angrier, the fact that I'm in contact with him or the fact that I'm in a relationship with a woman. Cassie being Uncle's housekeeper was just the last straw."

"So, did you tell her about the new project?"

"Which one? Oh, you mean *It Could Happen to You*."

"Obviously," he said, smiling at her.

"I told her that we want to try to get it into the US, and that we were hoping to ask Uncle Geraint about that."

"Are we?"

"Absolutely, why wouldn't we?" she asked.

"No reason. I just thought we should keep it to ourselves for a little longer."

"But not from my uncle, surely? I know it's your idea, but his input could be really useful."

"True," said Tenniel, giving her a sideways, slightly anxious glance, but she hardly noticed. She was still too preoccupied with thoughts of the lunch with her mother. Tenniel decided to drop the subject.

Chapter 3

Matt and Dilys stood to one side with Craig, who had insisted on staying to look after the dogs. He had them both on a lead, while they watched the white-suited SOCOs do their job. Photos had been taken, a search of the surrounding area had been made, and now they were waiting for Dr Pat Curtis, the regional pathologist, to arrive. Pat Curtis was not one of Matt's favourite people; a terse and sometimes rude woman, she was, nevertheless, very good at her job.

Matt wasn't at all sure the fall had been an accident, not because of anything he'd seen, he hadn't been close enough to the body to check – that was the job of the SOCO team and the pathologist. No, it was because of what Geraint had told him about the phone calls and e-mails. Had the person who'd made the threats been responsible for his death? If so, this was going to be one hell of a case, what with Geraint being famous worldwide. And then he thought of Fabia and his heart sank. She was going to be so upset, even if it was just an accident. She'd seen quite a lot of Geraint in the last couple of weeks and had grown very fond of him. Damn, damn, damn.

Dilys's mobile rang and Matt turned to listen as she answered it.

"Okay, let me just ask the chief." Still holding the mobile, she said, "Tom Watkins is at the gate and he says a car has just arrived, the woman driver says she's Geraint's housekeeper and she lives here. He's asking if he can let her through?"

"Just as far as the parking area. We can go round and meet her there."

She turned back to her call. "He says let her through, we'll come round and intercept her."

They left Craig guarding the dogs and walked round to the front of the house, arriving just as a white Fiat car screeched to a halt on the gravel. The young woman Matt had met when he'd visited Geraint jumped out of the car.

"What's going on? Why is there a policeman by the gate? What's happened?" The questions came thick and fast until she stopped to draw breath.

"You're Cassie Angel, Geraint's housekeeper?" Matt asked.

"Yes, yes, what's—"

But Matt interrupted her. "We'll explain everything. I'm Chief Inspector Lambert, here's my card, we met when I came to see Mr Denbigh a few weeks ago. This is my colleague Sergeant Bevan. Let's go into the house and I'll tell you why we're here."

Cassie frowned and Matt thought she was going to protest, but after a moment she turned and walked quickly to the front door, took out a key and unlocked it, and led them through to the sitting room. She pushed the door open and preceded them into a large room decorated in warm reds and greens. The polished wooden floor was covered with a magnificent Persian carpet and an ancient leather Chesterfield sofa stood at right angles to an elaborate marble fireplace. Several armchairs were also gathered in front of it.

Matt looked around and noticed that a half-moon table against one wall held two flowing sculptures of the human form; his eyes widened, he was sure they were Hepworths, or very much in her style, and almost every wall was covered in an eclectic mixture of photographs and paintings, just as Fabia had told him Geraint's study had been. It occurred to Matt that Geraint may have disturbed an intruder. There were certainly enough valuable artefacts in this house to attract burglars.

Cassie didn't sit down but paced up and down in front of the fireplace. "What the hell is going on?" she demanded.

Dilys went up to her and touched her arm. "Why don't we sit down, then the chief inspector can explain," she said.

For a moment Matt thought she would refuse, but then she threw herself into a chair and gripped the arms either side. Matt and Dilys both sat down, and Matt leant forward.

"I'm afraid we have bad news for you," he said.

"Is it Geraint?"

"Yes, it seems he fell from a window at the back of the house. The long one with the wrought iron round it."

"Oh God, I warned him. I kept telling him it was unsafe." She paused, her eyes widening. "Is he injured? Where is he?"

"I'm really sorry to have to tell you that he's dead," Matt said as gently as he could. "It seems he fell from the window in spite of the balcony."

"But it's not a balcony," she wailed. "Just a sort of safety guard thing, because the windows were down to the floor. I told him and told him it wasn't safe. Sorry, I'm babbling. But why are you here?"

"In a situation like this the police become involved until the exact cause of death can be established."

She stared at him for a moment as if she didn't understand what he'd said, then she jumped up. "I must tell Mari, she must know."

"Who is Mari?"

"My partner, Geraint's niece." She rummaged in one pocket then another. "Where's my phone? It must be in the car."

"I'll come and help you look for it," Dilys said, and followed her out of the room.

Matt stayed where he was, thinking about Geraint and the fact that he'd have to break the news to Fabia. And what if it was murder? That would make it even worse.

* * *

It wasn't until later that Cassie finally managed to contact Mari. When the call came through Mari was sitting at her desk concentrating on a storyboard on her computer screen. She glanced at her phone, saw who it was and smiled. A call from Cassie was always welcome.

"Hallo, my love," she said, "how's things?"

"Oh Mari," Cassie said, and immediately Mari knew that something was seriously wrong.

"What's up?"

"It's just so, so awful," Cassie said, a sob in her voice. "It's Geraint, he's... he's dead!"

"Oh God, no!" Mari exclaimed. "He can't be. He was fine when I saw him a couple of days ago. What happened? Has he had another stroke?"

"I don't know, they haven't let me see him. The gardener, Craig, found him early this morning."

"Where was he?"

"Out the back, under the apple tree," Cassie told her. "He always used to go for a wander round with the dogs after breakfast. I went to Cardiff first thing and he seemed fine when I left, but by the time I got back the ambulance was here, and the police. It looks as if he fell from the balcony in his bedroom. It needed fixing but I told him

23

not to try to do it himself, I *told* him. I'm so, so sorry, Mari."

"Is— is he still at the house?"

"No," Cassie told her, "the ambulance has just left, but the police are still here."

"Where's he been taken?"

"I don't know— no, maybe I do. They mentioned something about Royal Gwent Hospital, isn't that in Newport?"

"Yes." Mari could feel tears gathering in her throat. "Oh, Cassie, I want to see him; I want to say goodbye."

"But, Mari darling, do you think that's a good idea?"

"I'll phone the hospital," Mari insisted. "I must try and find out where he's been taken."

"I'm not sure they'll tell you."

"But I have to try." And nothing Cassie said could put her off.

* * *

"Mother? It's Mari. I've got some bad news, it's Uncle Geraint—"

"What's he done now?" Glenda asked dismissively.

Mari took a deep breath, tried to stay calm. "He's— he's dead." Her voice shook as she said it.

There was a moment of silence on the other end of the line, then her mother said, "I see. When did this happen? What happened?"

"Cassie just phoned me. He was found this morning just below the balcony in his bedroom." Mari didn't say anything about the police presence, but she wasn't quite sure why. She took a deep, steadying breath. "Mam, as his next of kin I need you to contact the hospital, find out where they've taken him. They won't tell me, they said it had to be the next of kin, and that's you."

"But why do you want to know, Mari?"

"I just— I just want— want to make sure it's true."

"Darling," her mother said, her voice more gentle now. "Isn't that a bit ghoulish?"

"Mother! Don't you care?" Mari demanded. "He is– was your brother, for God's sake!"

"I realise that, dear, and I'm very sorry, but you know we haven't been close."

"Is that all you have to say? How can you be so heartless?"

Again, there was a moment of silence, and then Glenda said, sounding resigned, "What hospital has he been taken to?"

"The Royal Gwent, in Newport."

"I'll contact them. And, Mari, I am sorry. I know how fond you were of your uncle."

"Thank you." Mari cut off the call and dropped her head in her hands, unable to stop the tears from coming.

She had been alone in the office, but Tenniel arrived back at that moment. He took one glance at her and hurried over, put a hand on her shoulder. "Mari, what's wrong?" he asked, sounding concerned.

She blew her nose, scrubbed at her eyes and looked up at him. "It's Uncle Geraint, he's had another stroke and he's– he's dead."

An expression that was hard to interpret flashed across Tenniel's face then was gone, so quickly that Mari hardly noticed. "How awful," he said. "When did it happen?"

"He was found this morning," Mari told him. "I've persuaded my mother to contact the hospital. I can't believe how cold she was about it, as if I was telling her about a stranger."

"But she's always been a bit like that about Geraint, hasn't she?" Tenniel said gently. "Not everyone gets on with their family members, look at my father and me." Tenniel had fallen out with his father as a teenager and hardly ever saw him.

"I suppose."

"Do you want to take the rest of the day off?"

"Would you mind? I want to go out and see Cassie, she's all on her own in that big house and she must be feeling lost."

"Off you go then, I'll hold the fort." He smiled at her and patted her shoulder.

She gathered up her coat and bag, gave him a quick hug and left the office. Once the door had closed, Tenniel stood staring across the empty office, an expression that was a mixture of anxiety and relief on his face.

Chapter 4

"Dr Curtis's report on Geraint Denbigh has just come in, sir," Dilys said as she came into Matt's office on Monday morning.

Matt sighed. "Here we go then. Let's have a look."

"I printed it out for you," Dilys said. She passed some sheets of paper across his desk.

Quickly he ran his eyes down the first page, then glanced up at Dilys who was standing looking worried and chewing at her bottom lip. He read on to the end.

Matt frowned at his sergeant. "She seems sure about it, doesn't she?"

"I haven't read it right through yet, just the first bit. She seems to have gone into a lot of detail, but then she usually does."

"She says here that the nature of the injuries to the upper torso make it look as if he was crushed against the wrought-iron Juliet balcony, guard rail whatever, before he fell. Apparently it's in need of repair and he could have been inspecting it. This" – he pointed to a particular part of the report – "about the nature of the head injury not being consistent with a fall, that's pretty conclusive. He was hit with something heavy and wedge-shaped. She thinks he might have been conscious after he fell and that the body was moved somehow."

"Moved? But why? The SOCOs didn't find any object of that description in the vicinity. But then, if he was murdered, whoever did it would have taken the weapon away. Stupid of me," Dilys said, tapping her hand to her forehead.

"Had you noticed this bit here, the bruising on the ankles? If he was leaning over the barrier, it wouldn't take much to grab him round the ankles and tip him over."

"I suppose," said Dilys. "And there's that bit about his being drugged. She says she's not sure what with, but she thinks he'd taken some kind of barbiturate. She's doing some more tests on that."

Matt glanced down at the report again. "Yes, you're right. And if anyone can identify a drug, Dr Curtis can."

Dilys smiled at this. "Very true, sir."

Matt was still looking at the report. "And what's this about rosemary in his hands? What do you think?"

"He could have picked it himself," Dilys said, but she didn't sound as if she believed this.

Matt grimaced. It was obvious he had his doubts too.

"Right. We must get the SOCOs out to the house again, see if they can find anything that might have been used as a weapon. And I want them to go over the wrought iron of the balcony again." He leant his elbows on his desk and dropped his head into his hands for a moment, then looked up at his sergeant. "Oh God, Dilys," he said. "Fabia's going to be really upset, it was bad enough when I told her that Geraint was dead, but this is really going to get to her."

"She was talking about him last time I spoke to her. He was very close to Fabia's aunt, wasn't he?"

"Yes, they were childhood sweethearts. He and Fabia spent a lot of time talking about her Auntie Meg." He pushed a hand through his hair and then sat back. "It wouldn't be so bad if it'd simply been another stroke, but this... this is different. I hope–"

A knock at his door interrupted their conversation and Matt looked up as it opened, then leapt to his feet.

"Good morning, ma'am," he said at the sight of his boss, Chief Superintendent Erica Talbot. Her cropped grey hair was neat, as was the rest of her slim figure, and her blue eyes were bright and sharp behind steel-rimmed glasses. Although short in stature, she had a presence about her which demanded respect.

Her appearance in Matt's office surprised him. This was not what he was used to. His previous boss, Charlie Rees-Jones, would never have deigned to come down to see Matt. He would have sent for him, tapping impatiently on his desk as he waited for Matt to rush upstairs.

"Morning, Chief Inspector; Sergeant," she said. "I just wanted a word about this report from the pathologist about Geraint Denbigh."

"Yes, I've just read through it."

Without invitation, she sat down opposite Matt's desk. "Pull up a chair, Dilys," she said. "I need you to be in on this as well."

Matt sat back down, wondering what was coming next. She appeared to be easy-going, but it had been made clear that she expected hard work and dedication – definitely the iron fist in a velvet glove approach. Now he waited for her to go on.

"It seems Dr Curtis is pretty certain of her diagnosis."

Matt nodded and waited for her to go on.

"You'll be SIO on this, Matt. Now, I gather your Fabia knew Geraint Denbigh well."

How on earth would she know that? Matt wondered, but he didn't ask, just said, "She does," and explained about Auntie Meg.

"I wonder if she'd be willing to come in and talk me through the background, his family and suchlike," his boss said, then added, with a small smile, "Don't look so shocked, Matt. I know the history, I've done my research, and although I haven't yet met her, from what I've heard I've developed a great respect for her."

All Matt could think of to say was, "Thank you, ma'am."

"Perhaps she could point us in the direction of those who may have wanted to harm him. What do you think?"

"I– er– I'm sure she'd be willing to help in any way she can," Matt said, thinking that Fabia would jump at the chance. "What do you think, Dilys?"

"I think she'd want to help out, after all, she has before, but…" Dilys trailed off, going a little pink, not sure whether she should have said so much.

"I told you about my meeting with Denbigh a couple of weeks ago, didn't I?" Matt said.

His boss nodded. "You did, and you said he'd sent you some further information."

"Quite a lot of it actually."

"Splendid. Well, perhaps you could have a word with Fabia and let me know what she says. We'll have to work quickly on this one, given his high profile. The media don't seem to have got wind of his death yet – the family seem to have kept it under wraps, or maybe the news of that cabinet minister caught with his kid's nanny kept them occupied." She gave them a cynical smile. "These people do come in useful sometimes."

Matt didn't comment, he hardly knew what to say.

The chief went on. "But now we know it is definitely murder we're dealing with it's bound to get out. They'll have an absolute field day, every hack in the book is sure to land up on our doorstep as soon as the news gets out. Let's get a press conference set up as soon as possible, tomorrow morning, I think. You and I can give them some titbits to be going on with and hope it keeps them under control."

"I'll get that organised," Dilys said, then reddened. "If that's okay with you, ma'am."

"Absolutely, Dilys, I'm sure you know what to do. So, best to get going don't you think?"

"Will do, ma'am," Matt said. What else could he say?

"I'm looking forward to meeting Fabia. I'd like to get to know her."

"I'm sure she'd– er– be pleased to hear that."

Erica Talbot gave Matt a slightly amused look, then got up and said, "Well, I'll leave you to it." She strode out of his office.

Matt sat back and stared across at Dilys. "Well, that's a turn-up for the books."

"I'll say. Do you think she's got some ulterior motive?"

"Who? The chief?"

"Yes– no, probably not." But Dilys was looking rather worried. "To be honest, like, I wonder if Fabia will be that keen."

"What, on meeting up with the new boss?"

"No, not so much that, but helping with the investigation. Won't she be too upset?"

"I don't know. Since she got pregnant, she's been a bit unpredictable."

"Par for the course, I think, if my sister is anything to go by," Dilys told him.

"I'll have to tread carefully."

"Why don't you go home for lunch?" Dilys suggested. "After all, that means you'll be halfway to Carreg Llwyd House, then we can meet you up there."

"I'm not sure, Dilys…"

"Go on, sir. The SOCOs have already done some of the job–"

Matt interrupted her, frowning. "I wonder how much will have been missed because we've lost those two days?"

"There's no way of knowing," Dilys said calmly. Keeping Matt from worrying too much had been one of her talents since they'd started working together. "We'll just have to get on with it now. I can tell Aidan Rogers he'll be needed. He says he's managed to retrieve most of those e-mails, which will be important evidence I'd say. I can get Sara Gupta, Dave Parry and Tom Watkins together, they're all in the office at the moment."

"What about Sharon?"

Dilys grimaced. Sergeant Sharon Pugh was not one of her favourite people. She was a chippy and difficult person who didn't take orders easily and, what was more, she and Fabia had clashed when they met during a case some months ago. "I'll keep her in reserve if that's okay with you. Remember how she dealt with Fabia last year?"

"I do indeed."

"Well, if Fabia's going to be involved," Dilys said, "we don't want a repeat of that behaviour."

Matt still hesitated. He really didn't think he should take time off, even one short hour, but the idea was very tempting. He wanted to be the one to tell Fabia that they'd be starting a murder inquiry. He didn't want her hearing about it from someone else before he got the chance to talk to her. And since the boss had suggested he ask for her help, couldn't that be thought of as an order?

"Okay," he said, grabbing his jacket from the back of his chair. "Can you get the press release sorted out as well, Dilys. You're good at that sort of thing." He chose to ignore the wry look Dilys gave him. "I'll go straight up to Carreg Llwyd House from home, as you suggest. I'll see you all up there in about an hour and a half."

Matt rummaged for his mobile as he strode out of his office and down the stairs. There was no reply from Fabia, so he texted her.

> I'm on my way home for lunch,
> have something to tell you,
> xxx Matt

* * *

Fabia unlocked the front door and hurried to the kitchen. She'd left her mobile on the table and she was worried that there might be a call or a message she'd missed. Unlike Matt she always made sure her phone was charged as she didn't like to be out of contact with the wider world. Glancing at the screen, she saw that there was a message, opened it and smiled. Matt very rarely came home at lunch time. After her initial doubts about Matt moving in, she now felt a buzz of pleasure that he called this house home now. Dropping her mobile into the pocket of her jeans, she went to investigate the contents of the fridge, got out some cold chicken, a box of various cheeses and a couple of jars of pickle, and then put a loaf of bread on the table as well.

Five minutes later Matt arrived home and came striding into the kitchen. Fabia swung round smiling, but one look at his face and the smile faded.

"What's wrong? Is it about Geraint?" she asked, going to him and putting her hand on his arm.

He put his arms round her and gave her a hug, then led her to a chair, sat down himself and took her hand in both of his, stroked at her fingers. "It's not good news, my love. I'm afraid Pat Curtis is pretty sure he was murdered. She says that the blow that killed him was administered after he'd fallen from the window, and there are a couple of other indications as well."

"Oh, no," she said, her voice agonised.

"Apart from the injuries, she's found traces of some barbiturate or other in his blood, so it looks as if he might have been drugged. She hasn't established which one yet." Matt paused, but Fabia said nothing. "I'm so sorry, but from the report it seems conclusive."

"Why does it always have to be murder? I don't want our child to be born into a world where every other death we come across is murder!"

"I know, I know. But, my lovely Fabia, it does come with the territory in my job doesn't it?"

She shrugged. "I suppose so."

"And there were those threatening e-mails and phone calls he told me about; he sent me quite detailed notes about them. Maybe it's something to do with those. Aidan is still busy trying to retrieve what he can. When I get back to the office, I must ask him how he's getting on."

Fabia got up and began to pace up and down, her arms clasped protectively round her body. Matt was used to this reaction. Stress always made her restless. Then she came back to her chair, cut some slices of bread and pushed the cheese and chicken towards Matt. "You'd better eat while you tell me the rest; every detail, mind."

Matt began to fill his plate. "What about you? Don't you want anything?"

"No, I couldn't."

"Fabia, you must eat," Matt said, frowning across at her.

"Matt! Leave it. Just tell me."

He did as she asked, told her that the report had come down from Chief Superintendent Talbot, that she'd appeared in his office to talk to him and Dilys about it, told him he'd be SIO and then left them to it.

"She came down to you?" Fabia said, distracted by this unusual behaviour.

"Yes." Matt gave a grimace. "A bit of a contrast to Rees-Jones."

"I'll say."

"But there's more, she said she'd been– how did she put it? She'd done some research into your past and has developed a great respect for you."

Fabia's eyebrows rose, but she didn't comment.

"She wants to meet up with you," Matt told her, "and she's asked if you'd be willing to advise us about Geraint's background, sort of bring us up to speed on him, his life and maybe his friends and enemies, I suppose she means. She pointed out that, given his high profile, once the press get hold of this we're going to be overrun by the media way beyond the usual, so the quicker we get going on the investigation the better, and the fact that you knew him could be very useful." He glanced up at Fabia as he said this and, seeing the pain in her eyes, put his hand across and clasped hers. "I'm so sorry, love. Would you rather not be involved?"

"No! I want to help. If this really is murder, I want to get the bastard." Fabia banged her fist down on the table. "Look, let me make a list of the names of a few people you should contact, people Geraint told me wouldn't be that pleased about his autobiography. Maybe one of them was involved."

"That'd be really useful. I can add it to the notes I've got already."

Fabia pulled forward a notebook that happened to be on the kitchen table, rummaged in her handbag for a pen, and began to jot down names. "I'll put down what they do as well," she told Matt, "you know, how and why he knew them, providing I know."

Matt nodded as he continued to eat his lunch and silence reigned for a while, the only sound the scratchy whisper of Fabia's pen.

After a few minutes of concentrated scribbling, Fabia looked up. "There you are, three or four of the worst offenders Geraint mentioned when it comes to shitty behaviour of various sorts." Fabia pushed the notebook across the table.

"For someone who was a bit of a recluse, he seems to have talked to you quite openly," Matt said.

"I suppose he did," Fabia replied, biting at her bottom lip. "We got on well. He was such a dear man." She frowned across at him. "Matt" – there was pleading in her voice – "do you really, really think it was murder?"

"I'm afraid so. Pat Curtis is usually right. Yes, I think we have a case."

"And it wouldn't have been self-administered," Fabia said firmly. "Not a drug like that."

"But that's not what killed him, although it might have made him less steady on his feet," Matt said as he laid down his knife and fork and glanced at his watch. "I'm

35

afraid I've got to get back to work. Dilys has been getting the team together and then we must meet the SOCOs up at the house." He came around the table and bent to kiss her. "Will you be okay?"

"Of course, I will," Fabia said with more confidence than she felt. "Apart from that list I've given you, you'll need to have a look through what he's written so far, in his autobiography I mean. It's going to be pretty revealing when it comes to people who may wish him harm. And another thing, Matt, you should get hold of Helen Tudor."

"The actress?" Matt said, recognising the name.

"Yes. They were very close friends and she may well have plenty of useful information. He told me he'd spoken to her quite recently."

"I'll add her to the list."

"And I expect Cassie, the housekeeper, will have plenty to tell you." She glanced at Matt's face and gave a rueful smile. "Of course, you would have thought of all that."

Fabia went with him to the front door and waved as Matt drove off, then closed the door and sagged against it as tears began to creep slowly down her cheeks. Then she pulled herself upright and dashed the back of her hand across her eyes. She'd become such a watering pot since she'd got pregnant. She told herself not to be such a wimp and strode back to the kitchen to put away the remains of Matt's lunch.

Chapter 5

Directly Matt got into his car he phoned Dilys and she quickly brought him up to date. "The SOCOs are on their way, and so are we. We'll probably get there about the same time as you. How was Fabia?"

"Upset, obviously, but very keen to 'get the bastard' as she put it. And she's already given me a list of people to watch out for. She's also suggested we interview Helen Tudor. Have you heard of her?"

"I have indeed," Dilys said. "She was magnificent in that BBC Wales series about Owain Glyndwr. She played his wife Margaret. Did you see it?"

"No, but I've seen her in several films. Fabia says she was a close friend of Geraint's. There's a portrait of her in his hallway."

"But she's not a suspect?" It sounded as if Dilys would be deeply shocked at the idea.

"No," Matt told her. "At least, not so far."

"And I got hold of Craig Evans, the gardener, he says he'll be at his parents' pub at four thirty so we can see him there."

When Matt got to the house there were a few people with cameras and recording equipment beginning to gather at the gate. He was followed very soon after by Dilys and the team. They parked on the gravel and Matt got out of the car and looked up at the grey granite house. Dilys came around to stand beside him.

"Impressive, isn't it?" she said. "But not exactly homely."

"No, but then it's more welcoming inside." Matt pointed to the corner of the house. "There are a few of those discreet cameras about the place, I noticed them when I came to see Denbigh a couple of weeks ago. I hope there's a good record kept of activities outside the house. It could be really useful."

"Definitely," Dilys agreed.

Matt turned to the others. "Let me know when the SOCOs arrive, meanwhile keep an eye."

As they stood there the front door opened to reveal the dark-haired, young woman they'd met two days before. Matt walked forward.

"I'm very sorry that we're having to disturb you again. Perhaps we could go inside, and I'll explain why we're back here."

She gave them a curt nod, hesitated a moment, then opened the door wider and they stepped into the hall. They followed her in, and she took them to the same room they'd been in before.

They settled themselves before the fire, which was unlit, and Cassie clasped her hands tightly in her lap.

"I don't really know why you should still be involved," she said, her voice low and troubled. "A fall from that height is bound to have– to have done a lot of damage."

Matt sat forward in his chair. He hated having to explain to family and friends that a death wasn't down to natural causes. It was bad enough for them to deal with and accept their loss, without adding the horror of murder.

"With a sudden death a post-mortem is usually carried out," he explained, "and I'm afraid, in Mr Denbigh's case, it has been established that it wasn't a simple fall, nor did he have another stroke. The pathologist has told us that she thinks he'd been drugged and then pushed over the balcony. The fall may not have killed him, but a subsequent injury to his head did."

Cassie gave a strange little moan and covered her face with her hands. They waited for her to recover herself.

"I– I don't believe it. How? Who would do such a thing to my dear Geraint?" Her eyes had filled with tears and she rummaged in the pocket of her jeans and brought out a creased tissue to wipe them away.

"You were very fond of him?" asked Dilys gently.

"Yes, yes, he was like an uncle to me. I've only been here for a couple of years but, well, we became very close."

"You weren't related then?" Matt asked.

"No, but it felt as if we were."

"How did you get the job?"

"Through an agency. He didn't want to advertise it openly in case he got a pile of paparazzi applying and then writing about him. Those people were always trying that sort of thing on him." She rummaged in a pocket for another tissue. "How could this have happened? I just can't believe it. He was so *kind*." The last word came out in a wail as she twisted the tissue to shreds in her fingers.

"We don't know yet, but that's what we are here to find out," Matt said. "We will need to have access to his computer, laptop and mobile phone, and any other devices he may have had. We'll also have to look through the recordings from the security cameras. Where do you keep them?"

"But didn't that policeman who came the other day look through all that?" she said, referring, Matt thought, to Aidan, the IT expert on the team.

"He did get some information, but a more in-depth search needs to be done. We need to retrieve as much information from the security cameras as possible." Matt paused then asked, "I gather Geraint was writing his autobiography."

"Yes. He'd nearly finished it. I was helping him. He wasn't very computer savvy and often got himself in a muddle. But lately he'd wanted to keep it more to himself, I think that might have been because..." – she paused, chewing at her bottom lip – "because he'd had some people objecting to the fact he was writing it, afraid of what he might say about them I suppose."

Matt glanced quickly at Dilys then asked, "Who were these people?"

"I'm not sure I should say."

"Cassie, may I call you Cassie?" Dilys asked.

"Yes."

"We need to know as much as we possibly can in order to discover who did this terrible thing. You are one of the people who could really help us. I'm sure you want to find Geraint's killer."

"Of course, I do. I'm sorry." Cassie looked from one to the other of them, her eyes anxious and pleading as she continued to twist her hands in her lap. "Please ask me anything you need to."

This was more like it. Matt sat forward in his chair. "Do you know of anyone who might wish to harm him?" he asked.

Cassie grimaced. "Several people. Geraint didn't suffer fools gladly and he was inclined to let it be known when he disapproved of someone. I think there are probably quite a few people who are wondering what will come out in his autobiography and, well, wondering probably isn't the right word, dreading more like."

"Why do you say that?"

"From what I've seen of it, parts of the autobiography are something of an exposé of certain people Geraint came up against in the film and television industry." She grimaced. "In a way I think he was using it to pay some people back for what he saw as past wrongs. With some of them he certainly had reason."

"Can you think of anyone in particular?" Matt was watching her carefully as he asked the question, wondering as he did so if these people would be on Fabia's list.

"Well, two men come to mind immediately, and they've both been to visit Geraint recently. They might have been more than once, I don't know. The first is an agent that Geraint had dealings with years ago, a man called Brandon Gaunt, I think they fell out over a woman, and the other is a director called Stephen Lowe. Geraint said something to me about the #MeToo movement being interested in both of them."

Matt could tell, from her tone of voice, that she disliked both men. He gave no sign whether or not the names were familiar to him, instead he homed in on one particular thing she'd said. "And you say both of these men came to see him recently?"

"Yes. I could look up the exact dates in Geraint's diary. He was always meticulous about noting down who visited, providing he knew in advance. Sometimes he made a note of it anyway."

"Why do you think that was?" Dilys asked.

"I think it was because he found it difficult to trust anyone and wanted proof that they'd been here in case they passed anything to the media and he needed to tackle them," Cassie said. "He was obsessed with trying to control the media's interest in him, which is hardly surprising. He said they were always telling lies about him. He probably wasn't far wrong."

"We'll have to take the diary for checking—"

"Yes, I suppose you will," she said, frowning.

Using the gentle tone she'd used before, Dilys said, "As part of our investigation into his death, we'll have to look through all Mr Denbigh's private papers. It's standard procedure in a case of this nature."

The blood drained from Cassie's face and Matt thought it was the first time she'd truly faced the fact that this was a murder inquiry. He felt sorry for her, all alone in this rambling house with no-one to support her. Although his team would be on site for some time, it was hardly the same as having someone you knew around to keep you company.

"Do you have anyone we can call to be with you?" Dilys asked, she'd obviously had the same thought. "This must be very difficult for you. It would be good to have a friend or relative with you."

"I've got no relatives close by, but I do have a girlfriend. It's Mari Reynolds, Geraint's niece, she'll be coming round later, but I think I'll probably be doing the supporting. We'll look after each other, she means a lot to me." She gave them a sad little smile, then her expression changed to one of alarm. "The day he died, I phoned her and told her, but I don't think she knows– knows about you being here. That you think he was killed by someone. She'll be at work."

"Where does she work?" Matt asked.

"In Cardiff. She has a production company. I'd better phone her."

"We can send someone round to inform her. We'll obviously have to speak to his family and close friends during the course of the investigation." Matt paused then asked, "Do you know of anyone who has visited lately who may wish Mr Denbigh harm?"

Cassie frowned and chewed at a thumbnail, then said, "Other than the two I've already mentioned, no, not really, although Helen Tudor was here a few days ago." She gave them a quick glance under her brows, then added, diffidently, "I think she and Geraint had a bit of a row."

"A row?" Matt said. "Do you know what it was about?"

"No. I just heard raised voices and soon after that she left. She looked a bit mad."

"Mad?" Matt asked.

"Sorry, cross." Cassie grimaced. "I watch too much American TV."

Matt stored away what she'd said about Helen Tudor and resolved to speak to her as soon as he could.

At this moment they were interrupted by a knock at the door. It opened and DC Sara Gupta came into the room. "Excuse me, sir, but I thought you ought to know that the SOCO team is here, and Aidan Rogers is on his way."

"Thank you, Sara, I'll be out in a minute." He turned back to Cassie. "Could you give us the address for Ms Reynolds, and her mobile number, please?"

Cassie pushed herself forward and got up. "But I'd prefer to–"

Dilys and Matt both stood up.

"I think it would be best if one of our team spoke to her first," Matt said firmly. He turned to Dilys. "Would you take care of that, please?" Then he turned back to Cassie. "I'm sure she'll contact you once we've done so. We might want to speak to you again, but we must get to work now. I wonder if you could show my sergeant where Mr Denbigh's computer is, and his laptop as well, please?"

She hesitated, frowning, and Matt thought she was about to protest, then her shoulders sagged, and she said to Dilys, "They're in the study. I'll show you."

"And perhaps you could show her where the security camera records are kept."

Cassie simply nodded and Dilys followed her out while Matt crossed the hall and left the house by the front door. There were two SOCO vans parked in the driveway and several white-suited personnel were in evidence. Matt looked around for the team leader and spotted her standing by one of the vans. He was pleased that it was someone he'd worked with before. Karen Johns was a talented and efficient forensics expert who'd been in charge when Geraint's body was found.

"Good afternoon, Chief Inspector," she said at sight of Matt. "I hadn't expected to be back here so soon. Any more useful information for me? It's a great shame that we didn't have the pathologist's report before, but that's expecting rather too much, even of Pat Curtis."

"It is," he said, smiling at her. "I think Sergeant Bevan has given you everything we have so far," Matt said. "Mr Denbigh's housekeeper, Cassie Angel, is at home. Could you let your team know that?"

"Will do," she said, then turned to one of her colleagues.

Matt watched as they disappeared round the back of the house followed by other members of the team.

As he stood there, a shaven-headed giant of a man levered himself out of a small car that had just arrived. Matt wondered why Aidan Rogers hadn't thought to buy himself a larger vehicle, given his height and girth.

"Afternoon, sir," he said as he approached. "What have you got for me?"

"The computer is where it was when you last had a look at it, so start with that. You need to have another look at his laptop, and there's his phone of course. That was retrieved from the body after it was found." Matt nodded towards Sara who was standing waiting for instructions. "Sara will tell you where everything is."

"I've never dealt with someone famous before, it–"

"There's no difference to anyone else, Aidan," Matt said repressively.

Aidan nodded, unabashed. "Okay, sir, I'll get going." He followed Sara into the house.

Matt grimaced. They were going to have a lot of that curiosity about Geraint. He'd have to watch out for it amongst his staff.

As he and Dilys drove back down the drive they passed an outside broadcast van, a television crew and the small crowd of men and women, cameras in hand, faces sharp and enquiring, who'd been gathered at the gate when they arrived. They all craned to look, eager to find out who was in the car. Dilys took out her mobile and keyed in Tom's number.

"Just to warn you, Tom, the press are gathering. And we'll need more from uniform, could you arrange that?"

"Bloody nuisance," Matt muttered as they turned into the road and headed for Pontygwyn and The Oaks pub to interview Craig Evans.

"I asked Sara to go and keep Ms Angel company, sir. She's done her family liaison training, so it'll be good practice for her."

"You're right, I'd forgotten that." He glanced at Dilys. "Feels like going back four years when we thought Craig might have been involved in the Morgan case."

"It does," said Dilys. "There's been a lot of water under the bridge since then."

"I'll say. And since then I've changed my mind about the boy, he's a hard worker, is Craig. Does a great job on Fabia's— our garden. That reminds me, I must try to get home at a reasonable time this evening. I've been late so often recently that Fabia says she'd beginning to forget what I look like."

"Are you still in trouble over missing the antenatal class?" Dilys asked.

Matt smiled. "No, I don't think so. I made it up to her. It's no good giving Fabia flowers, she says they should be in the garden, not in a vase, so I went and bought her a clematis plant from that garden centre between Usk and Llangybbi. She's been wanting one for ages."

"Nice thought. Well done. Next time Susan and I have a row I hope she does the same, I'll drop some hints."

Chapter 6

At the Armitages' house near Caerleon, Glenda was waiting impatiently for her husband, Jonathan, to arrive home. He'd sent her a text to say he was on his way, and given that it was Monday, the traffic shouldn't be too bad. But still she couldn't settle to anything. He'd flown back from a meeting in Geneva to stay at the London flat the night before and had told her that everything was fine, the meeting had gone well, but Glenda was still worried. When they'd spoken, he'd sounded preoccupied, and was curt, which wasn't like him. Although he wasn't the warmest of people, he was always polite.

Yet again she looked out of the sitting room window to the driveway and the road beyond and relief flowed through her as, this time, she saw his Mercedes turn in at the gate and park on the neatly paved driveway. Putting a hand up to her chest, she took a few deep breaths. She knew from experience she mustn't show Jon how worried she'd been, he hated to see her stressed. But she couldn't stop herself from going to the front door to open it before he'd even had the chance to drag his small suitcase from the boot of the car.

"Hallo, darling," Glenda said, keeping her voice light and unconcerned. She hadn't told him that she thought Geraint might have been murdered. She'd told herself she didn't want to burden him while he was busy. And even now she was still inclined to put it off. "How was the drive? Lots of traffic?"

"Not that bad," he said as he bent to kiss her cheek, but it was an absent-minded gesture.

Glenda felt tension rising inside her again. Jon was ten years her junior and, sensitive to his every mood, she worried constantly that she would lose him to a younger woman, someone he could easily meet on one of his frequent business trips to Europe or the USA. As he walked past her into the hall and put his suitcase down, she could tell he was not his usual self.

He turned and asked, "Is there any more news about Geraint?"

She felt a churning in her stomach at the thought of what she suspected. He was probably just worried about Geraint's death and how it would affect her. After all he, unlike her, had got on quite well with her brother and had always questioned her attitude, implying that it would be better to stay on good terms given Geraint's high profile.

"Never mind your suitcase, we can take it up later," Glenda said. "Come into the kitchen, I'll make us some tea and bring you up to date on what's been happening. I'm afraid there's some rather worrying news."

He didn't seem to have taken this in as he followed her into the light and airy kitchen at the back of the house, with its gleaming stainless steel double-doored fridge, its top-of-the-range cooker and expensive labour-saving gadgets. The granite worktops gleamed, and a large vase of lilies filled the room with their heavy scent.

Glenda reached into a cupboard for mugs, switched on the kettle, and then turned to Jon who had hoisted himself up on to a tall stool at the kitchen island.

"Actually, darling," Jon said, running a hand over his neat grey hair, "could you pour me a gin and tonic rather than tea. I feel in need of one."

"Oh?" Her worries swept back. This was unusual for John. "Isn't it a bit early?"

"Come on, Glenda. I'll fix it if you don't want to."

"No, no, I'm happy to do it." She went to the fridge and got out a bottle of tonic, put a glass under the ice dispenser then reached for the gin. A tense silence reigned until she'd put his drink in front of him and made herself some tea. Finally, she took a stool opposite him and said, "I've got a lot to tell you."

"Okay. You said on the phone that there was news, and it didn't sound good to me."

"It isn't. The police want to come and talk to us."

"The police?" His hand jerked and some of the contents of his glass slopped onto the granite top of the island. He didn't seem to notice, just snapped, "Why on earth?"

"They didn't say exactly, but they'll be here later. A post-mortem was done, on Geraint I mean, but– but I don't know if that's got anything to do with it."

He stared across at her, but she looked quickly away. "Glenda! What are you implying?"

She didn't give him a direct answer. "You know Geraint was writing his autobiography," she said.

He just nodded.

"Well, there are plenty of people who'd want to stop him doing that, afraid of what he might say about them, and I was wondering if one of them decided to– to actually stop him."

"You mean do him harm? Why on earth would you think that?"

Glenda looked up at him and was shocked that he had paled and, for a second, she thought there was fear in his eyes. Why? What was he afraid of? Then she remembered a conversation they'd had a couple of weeks ago. Jon had told her that they were having a few money problems. He'd made light of it, insisted it was purely temporary, putting it down to some investments going through troubled times. She mustn't worry, he would sort it all out, but he'd asked her to try to keep their expenses down for a while, just until he'd worked out how serious the situation was. And she also remembered that he'd said he was going to speak to Geraint to find out if he could give them some temporary help. She'd protested, told him her brother wouldn't consider it, but Jon had insisted.

Before she could stop herself, she blurted out, "Jon, did you speak to Geraint about those investments?"

"What investments?"

But she was sure he knew what she was talking about. "You said we had to be careful, for a while."

Glenda had never been involved in their finances. She'd always had an aversion to dabbling, as she called it, in money, although she'd never been averse to spending it. As a consequence, she knew little about Jon's life in the finance industry or how exactly he made his money. "You told me you were going to ask him for help," she said. "Did you? Did he refuse?"

Jon glanced at her then away again, drained his glass and went to mix himself a refill. He didn't sit down again but went and stood looking out of the window at the neat garden outside, his back to her. "I did go and see him, just before I went back up to London. He refused point blank to help in any way at all. He was particularly brisk about it."

"But what else did you expect, he–"

"I thought he just might give me a temporary loan, for the sake of the family."

Glenda made a derisive noise. "You have to be joking. Not my brother!"

Jon turned to look at her. "I've never had the same view of him as you, not until now, and since he's so fond of Mari I thought he might stump up, since he gave her so much help."

"Mari? What help?"

"Did she not tell you?" Jon smiled, but there was a mocking edge to it. "You really should learn to communicate with your daughter even if you couldn't do so with your brother."

A flush rose in Glenda's face. "That's not fair, Jon. And you haven't answered my question."

"Mari told me quite a while ago, when I offered to help with the finances for Cariad Productions, that because Geraint had invested some money in the company she didn't need my help. Turned me down flat, very politely." This time his smile had a sardonic twist to it. "She's always very polite to me."

Glenda ignored this comment and stuck to the subject uppermost in her mind. "How long ago was it that you went to see him?"

"Oh, about four weeks ago."

"Things have been bad for that long?" Glenda exclaimed, a note of panic in her voice. "What is happening, Jon? I wish you'd explain to me why we've got money problems. You never tell me anything."

"Because you don't really want to know, do you?"

"I do if we're in trouble."

For a few moments there was silence, then Jon gave his wife a sharp glance, took a deep breath and said quietly, "Anyway, the problem may not exist for very much longer."

"What do you mean?" Glenda held her breath. Relief rose inside her.

"When I went to see Geraint about the money, he said we'd have to wait until he died before we got our hands on his money. He told me that in spite of the fact you hated his guts – his words – he was leaving virtually everything to you and Mari between you, other than a few bequests to close friends and to Cassie. You, my darling, will be a very rich woman once probate is through. I'd say that's our problems sorted!"

He didn't get the reaction he was expecting. All the blood drained from Glenda's already pale face as she stared across at him.

"But– but, Jon–" she said, her voice a thread of its usual sharp tone.

He frowned, then demanded, "What's the matter with you, Glenda?"

"I told you, the police are coming to speak to us. I've been thinking about it all afternoon and this awful idea occurred to me. What if they think Geraint was– was killed?"

"What? Do you mean murdered?"

"To shut him up, what if–"

"For Christ's sake, Glenda, you have to be joking." He gave a bark of derisive laughter, but there was no humour in it.

* * *

Dusk was falling as Matt and Dilys parked outside the Armitages' house.

"I'd say there's a tidy bit of money been put into this place," Dilys remarked as they got out of the car. "I remember coming by here with my mam when I was a kid, it was almost derelict then, a tumble-down old farmhouse with very little to recommend it."

"It's certainly not that now," Matt said as they walked towards the front door.

Matt gave a sharp rap on the brass knocker and, a moment later, the door was opened by a square-jawed man with neat grey hair.

"Good evening, I'm Chief Inspector Lambert, Newport police," Matt said, holding out his identification, "this is my colleague, Detective Sergeant Bevan."

"Jon Armitage," the man said, and opened the door wider. "My wife said we should expect you. Come in."

They followed him through to a large sitting room, expensively furnished but rather impersonal. There were no family photos scattered about, no clues to the owners and their relatives, just a room that could have been part of any up-market hotel or the subject of a glossy magazine article. As they entered, a slim, neatly dressed woman rose from a chair by a white marble fireplace. She clasped her arms across her body in an unconsciously protective gesture.

"The police are here, my dear," Jon said. "This is my wife, Glenda. Shall we sit, and you can tell us why you want to speak to us." He was very much in charge.

Although they sat side by side, Matt noticed the Armitages didn't seem relaxed with each other. She sat back in her chair and, after one quick glance at her husband she turned away; he'd chosen a chair to the side so that they weren't facing each other. Matt wondered if this was deliberate, then told himself he was probably over-thinking it all. Dilys, as usual, chose an upright chair to the side and took out her trusty notebook while Matt took a seat opposite the couple.

"So, what is it you need to speak to us about?" Jon asked, his tone brisk, and Matt wondered how much his wife had told him. "I'm only just back from Geneva and I have another important meeting in London first thing tomorrow."

Matt had asked Sara Gupta to do some research into the Armitages. She'd discovered that Jon Armitage worked for a hedge fund company called Apudo Holdings which was based in the City of London with offices in Kenya and the Cayman Islands. She had also discovered that the Financial Conduct Authority was looking into some of their activities, insider dealing and tax evasion had been mentioned.

"Given how busy I am," Jon continued briskly, "I'd be grateful if we could get things cleared up as speedily as possible."

Matt gave Dilys a quick glance then decided to deal with this assertive man in his own way. For a moment no-one spoke. Matt let the silence drag out a little. Glenda Armitage sat with her hands clasped tight in her lap and Matt was sure she was clenching her teeth. Her husband was much cooler, but Matt thought a lot of effort was going into maintaining the calm façade.

Matt looked straight at him. "The speed at which we can deal with the situation, sir, is dependent on various factors," he said firmly. "I'm afraid I have some bad news for you."

There was a tightening of Glenda Armitage's hands, but her husband merely raised an eyebrow.

Matt went on. "With a sudden death, as is the case with your brother, Mrs Armitage, we ask for a post-mortem. This has been done and the pathologist has established that your brother did not die of natural causes, he was murdered."

Glenda Armitage gave a small choking sound and put a hand up to her mouth but said nothing, just gave her husband a look that was full of fear. Jon Armitage put out a hand and clasped hers. Matt could tell it was not a gentle gesture.

"Are you sure of this?" he asked.

"Yes, we are," Matt told him.

His wife opened her mouth to speak but Jon got in first. "But who on earth would do such a thing? Do you think theft was involved? He's got a lot of valuable artwork in that house. He must have interrupted an intruder or something. That's the most likely thing to have happened." It was as if he could make it be so by stating it as a fact. "When did this happen?"

Matt was surprised at the question. Surely his wife had already told him. But he answered without revealing his thoughts. "His body was found last Friday and the result of the post-mortem came through this morning," Matt told him. "As you say, your brother-in-law owned some very valuable artwork. Quite apart from anything else, a thief would also have been interested in televisions, laptops, they're easy to sell on. But, as far as we can establish so far, nothing was stolen."

Matt waited for their reaction to this. It came in a rush from Glenda Armitage, going off at a tangent. "My brother was writing his autobiography and I'm sure he wasn't going to hold back when it comes to people who crossed him. He never did."

"In what way?" Matt asked.

"He had some very dubious friends in America, and in London I dare say, and he could be pretty spiteful at times. He would have enjoyed telling the world about other people's secrets and peccadilloes."

From her tone Matt got the impression she'd be on the side of the dubious friends rather than her brother.

"What's to stop them travelling to Wales to confront him?" Glenda asked. "It was probably someone like that, someone who was afraid of what he might reveal."

"That's a strong possibility," Jon said. "Have you investigated that angle? Geraint had a pretty efficient security system so, as you've said, you can rule out burglary."

"We will be addressing this case from every angle, but it's early days yet," Matt said. "Have you any idea who these friends might be?" Matt directed his question at Glenda Armitage.

"No, I haven't," she said sharply. "I had very little to do with my brother or his friends. His private life was his own affair and I preferred not to know anything about it."

"I think what my dear wife means," Jon said, with a deprecating smile, "is that we saw little of Geraint. He came back to Wales a few years ago, but he was a bit of a recluse. And we don't spend all our time here, so there was little opportunity, unfortunately, to get together."

"I could have if I'd wanted to, but I didn't," she muttered.

"Yes, my dear. But Mari kept us up to date with how he was doing, they were very close."

"Mari is your daughter?" Matt asked.

"Yes," Glenda Armitage said. She began to chew at her lip, looking less sure of herself now, and Matt wondered if she'd realised her attitude wasn't coming across well. "He, my brother, was a very private person. We weren't close, but that doesn't mean I wished him harm, of course I didn't." She glared at Matt as if he'd accused her of wishing just that.

"I think you should concentrate your investigation on the many people in Geraint's work life who could have worried about what he would put in his autobiography, as my wife suggested," Jon said firmly.

"Could you give me the names of any of those people?" Matt asked.

"How would we know their names?" Glenda asked sharply. "As I just said, I didn't know much about my brother's private life." She then added, "I suppose there was that actress woman, Helen Tudor, I think they were more than friends at one time. I gather they fell out in a big way, it was all over the tabloids. And there could be hundreds of others that he got on the wrong side of, that was the sort of person he was."

Her husband frowned across at her, his lips tight, his eyes cold. It was obvious that he was far more aware of the bad impression she was making than she was.

"I'm sure you understand that my wife is very upset. This has been a terrible shock to all of us. Mari, my stepdaughter, was particularly close to Geraint and Glenda has been trying to comfort her. As you can imagine, that has added to the... the burden of grief."

"We understand, sir," Matt said smoothly. "We'll leave you in peace now. Thank you for your co-operation. We will probably need to speak to you again as the investigation progresses."

"Why?" asked Glenda Armitage sharply as she rose from her chair, arms clasped tight across her chest.

"Because," Matt said patiently, "you may remember something that you feel is relevant, that will help us with our enquiries."

"I think I know what that means," she said with a tight little smile.

"Glenda," her husband said, a warning note in his voice, "you must let the chief inspector do his job. Surely you want to know who did this dreadful thing."

"Yes, yes, of course." She put a hand up to her mouth and gazed at Matt over her fingers, her eyes full of fear, then she took a deep breath and said, "I'm sorry, Chief Inspector. As my husband says, this is all so very upsetting."

Jon escorted them to the front door and said, quietly, as they stood on the doorstep, "I'm sure you understand what a shock this has been for my wife."

"Of course, sir," Matt assured him. "We'll make sure we keep you both informed of our progress."

Matt turned to make his way down the steps, but before he did so he turned back. Jon was still standing in the doorway as if to make sure they left. Keeping his voice conversational, Matt said, "One more thing, sir. Am I right in thinking that you work for Apudo Holdings?"

The man frowned and a wary expression came into his face. "Yes, I'm the director in charge in London."

"Some information has come through to us from the FCA that there is an on-going investigation into the company, is that correct? Something to do with insider dealing and possibly tax evasion."

"Your information is correct in that there is an investigation," Jon said, his voice cold as steel. "If you had done a little more research, you would have discovered that it's a case of a disenchanted employee we were forced to let go; he started this rat running but it will come to nothing."

"Thank you, Mr Armitage. I will do as you suggest and carry out further research. Good evening to you."

But Jon wasn't finished. "Hold on a moment, Chief Inspector. Tell me again, when was Geraint – er – killed?"

"Last Friday."

"That's what I thought you said. In order to help you with your enquiries and eliminate possible suspects" – he gave Matt a slightly twisted, humourless smile – "I was in Geneva for the whole of last week, I only got back yesterday and stayed in our London flat last night as I was meeting a friend for dinner. I can give you his name and address if you wish."

"That won't be necessary at the moment, sir. Perhaps you could tell us which hotel you were staying at and what your business was in Geneva?"

Armitage rattled off the information and Dilys jotted it down.

"Thank you, sir," Matt said.

As they drove away, Dilys turned to Matt. "You put the cat among the pigeons there, sir, but I think he felt he'd got the better of us in the end."

"He probably did, arrogant bugger," Matt said. "Let him stew, though, when it comes to his financial dealings. It could have no relevance to the case, but people like him irritate me."

"I think I could tell that," Dilys said with a smile, then she changed the subject. "That is a very frightened woman."

"You're not wrong, but why?"

"What is it called when you kill a sibling?"

"Fratricide, I think. So that's what you think we're dealing with?"

"Could be," Dilys said, "could be."

"But I wouldn't think she'd be strong enough to push – well, lift – her brother over that balcony railing. She's such a dab of a woman."

"Perhaps not, but she could have had help."

Matt frowned. He hadn't thought of that.

Chapter 7

Several miles away, at Carreg Llwyd House, Cassie and Mari sat close together in Cassie's small sitting room on the first floor. It was cosy and warm, and they'd retreated up there to get away from the police activity downstairs. Chester and Jasper, the two Dobermanns, sat on a rug in front of the fireplace, both awake and alert but obedient to Cassie's order to stay quiet. Cassie's arm was round Mari's shoulders and she stroked at her neck with soft fingers.

"It's so awful," Mari said. "It'd be bad enough if he'd had another stroke, but murder! I really don't think the police can be right. Quite apart from anything else, who could have got into the house while you were out? Geraint probably would have ignored the bell if it had rung, and the dogs would have set up a racket."

"I know what you mean," Cassie agreed, "but they seemed pretty sure of it. Did they tell you what the post-mortem report said exactly?"

"No, just that they were treating it as a suspicious death and that there'd be an inquest where we'd find out more. They also said they'd keep me informed of their progress." Mari put her hands up to her face. "Oh God, Cassie," she said, her voice muffled behind her fingers, "I'm going to miss him so much."

"I know, I know," Cassie said softly.

"The thing is, Geraint had mentioned that he was going to try to fix the railing and I said not to," Mari said. "I told him to ask the gardener bloke, what's his name?"

"Craig."

"To ask him to do the repair, but you know what my uncle was like, always wanted things done now if not sooner."

"Didn't he just," Cassie said, smiling. "I told him the same, and he did say he wouldn't attempt it without help, but we both know what he was like."

"And if he tried to do it himself, he might have over-balanced and fallen, mightn't he?"

Cassie's eyes widened. "You could be right."

"I think I'd better mention it to that chief inspector because they might not have thought of that, and it may make a difference to how they… how they approach it all. I'd rather he wasn't dead at all, but murder seems so much worse than an accident, doesn't it?"

Cassie put both her arms round Mari and hugged her tight. "Yes, it does." She sat back. "Now I'm going to go and fix us something to eat. Are you going to stay here tonight? I'd so love your company."

"Of course I will, and I'll come and give you a hand. I need something to do."

* * *

Matt got home at half past eight, tired and hungry. As he opened the front door the rich smell of a chicken casserole wafted down the hallway and, throwing his coat onto a chair in the hall, he strode through to the kitchen to find Fabia. She was sitting at the table sketching on a pad and, as was often the case when she was concentrating on a drawing, she didn't notice him come in. He stood looking at her for a moment, her elbow on the table, forehead resting on her hand with fingers thrust into her curly hair, and the scratch, scratch of the charcoal she was using the only sound. A wave of love swept over Matt and he strode forward, pulled her from her chair, and kissed her.

Fabia responded with enthusiasm then pulled back. "What was all that about?" she asked, smiling at him and stroking his cheek.

"Just wanted to show you how much I love you," he said, pulling her back into his arms, but she wriggled away.

"No, no, supper first and then an update. The casserole's ready and I've done baked potatoes. I'll get the plates and cutlery, you get the food out of the oven. You can bend over more easily than me."

She began to clear the pad and pieces of charcoal away and Matt glanced across at what she'd been drawing.

"Is that Geraint?" he asked.

"Yes, bless him. I just felt like getting it down while he was in my mind. It's therapeutic."

"And an excellent likeness."

"Do you think so?" Fabia asked, sounding pleased. "It's not finished yet."

"But you've already got those lean lines and slightly hooded eyes just right."

"Thank you," Fabia said, and Matt noticed that there were tears in her eyes.

"Come on then, let's get this food on the table," he said in an effort to distract her. "I haven't eaten in hours and I'm famished."

"For goodness sake, you had all that lunch. It's so unfair that you can eat as much as you like and stay skinny." She rubbed at her rounded tummy. "I'm so fat."

"You're not fat, that's Thumper, so stop fussing," Matt said, smiling at her.

A few minutes later they were sitting down to their meal and Fabia said, "Now, tell me what's been happening?"

As they ate Matt brought her up to date on what Cassie had told them. "Then she phoned later on and told us that the balcony Geraint fell from was unsafe, something about the wrought-iron railings coming away from the brickwork. But we knew that already, the SOCOs had pointed it out and Craig had mentioned it."

"You saw him this afternoon?"

"Yes, and he was very useful." Matt poured himself some wine and topped up Fabia's glass of water. "Craig's been doing the gardening there for a while now, most mornings. He told us that Geraint has had more visitors lately than he used to."

"Yes, he told me about it," Fabia said.

"The thing is, Craig says he overheard a couple of conversations that could be relevant. By the way, did you know he wants to apply to join the force?"

"No! But what an excellent idea, he'd be really good."

"Do you think so?" Matt said, his tone a little doubtful.

"Absolutely. He's very observant, did you know he has a photographic memory?"

"No, that could be useful."

"I know," Fabia said, "and with his past he'll have some understanding of the toerags he'd be dealing with on the beat."

"You mean he's been there, done that?"

Fabia smiled. "Yes, but nothing serious in his case. I do hope he's accepted."

"You could put in a word for him. I suggested he ask you to be one of his referees."

"I'd be delighted," said Fabia. "But come on, that's for another time, what did he tell you about these visitors?"

"He says the first one was three weeks ago. He saw this bloke drive up in a top-of-the-range Jaguar." Matt grinned. "Craig definitely remembers the car."

"He's always been car and motorcycle mad," Fabia said. "I remember Dilys remarking on a motorbike he used to own a few years ago."

"The Yamaha, yes. Anyway, he was in the front garden when the man arrived and asked Craig if this was Geraint's house. He said he had an American accent and he was big and muscular, white-haired and wore glasses. Cassie had mentioned two people that we might be interested in, a director called Stephen Lowe and an agent called Brandon Gaunt, and Geraint mentioned them both to me when I saw him about the e-mails and texts. Craig said the other visitor was only last week and described him as Italian-looking, dark receding hair and very posh clothes. He said he was so smooth he was surprised the clothes didn't slither off him, which I thought was a great description."

"Did you download photos of Gaunt and Lowe after you spoke to Geraint?" Fabia asked.

"Yup, and Craig identified both of them."

"Good for him."

"The first one, the American, was Brandon Gaunt, a film and theatrical agent, and the second visitor was Stephen Lowe, who's a British director who's worked over in the US but does most of his work in the UK."

"So, how much did Craig overhear?" Fabia asked, impatient for more information. "What were the arguments about?"

Matt didn't give her a direct answer. "Although he didn't actually say so, I'm pretty sure Craig made a point of eavesdropping. I got the impression he felt protective of Geraint, he certainly liked him, said he was a top bloke. And he definitely didn't take to this Gaunt character."

"So, what did he overhear?"

"He said he was digging up the bed below the study window and he heard mention of Geraint's autobiography. They were talking quite quietly at first, but then he heard the agent bloke shout 'You bastard! You can't do that'. He couldn't hear Geraint's response, it was just a soft murmur, and then there was more shouting from Gaunt, something about 'I'll see you in hell first' and 'You'd better watch yourself, one of these days you're going to end up dead'.

Soon after that, he heard the front door slam and, when he looked out towards the front of the house, the Jaguar was screeching down the drive and out on to the road."

"But it's just the sort of thing anyone might say in a temper," Fabia said, playing devil's advocate.

"True, but it still gives us a reason for having a word with this Gaunt bloke."

"What about the other one, Stephen Lowe?" Fabia asked.

"Come on. I'll make some coffee then we can go into the sitting room and get comfortable and I'll tell you the rest," Matt said.

"Good idea. I lit the fire earlier on. It was getting chilly."

Once settled on the slightly shabby but comfortable sofa in front of the glowing logs in the fireplace, Matt continued his account.

"Where's this Stephen Lowe from?" Fabia asked.

"London, I think, though it seems he has a house in Newmarket. He's into horses, owns a couple apparently," Matt told her.

"I know someone in the Suffolk police, we worked on a drugs bust together, I think it was around 2010. With any luck she might still be there. I could have a quiet word. It'd probably be quicker than going through the usual channels."

Matt laughed. "I don't think there's any force where you don't have some kind of contact somehow."

"It's called networking, Matt," Fabia said, raising a mocking eyebrow.

He didn't rise to the bait. "And you're very good at it."

"Craig said Lowe looked like some rich gangster. This time the car was a Rolls – I was given a detailed description of it, a pale grey Rolls Royce Phantom. He told me how much it would have cost, it's top speed, everything. Like you said, Craig is really into his cars."

Fabia grinned but didn't comment.

"Craig remembers that it was exactly a week before he found Geraint's body because that was the day he was earthing up his new potatoes," Matt said. "Very precise, is Craig, keeps a gardening notebook with the jobs he does listed in it."

"I know. He's methodical and organised, bless him."

"Anyway, when Lowe knocked there was no response, and Cassie was out, so Craig said he'd go and find out if Geraint was in. He found him out the back, sitting on the terrace, and apparently the man had followed him round, hadn't waited to find out if he was welcome, which annoyed Geraint somewhat." Matt took a gulp of his coffee. "Craig said he made himself scarce but didn't go far as it was obvious Geraint didn't want this smooth bloke around. He said he could hear little of their conversation at first but, as with Gaunt, it got a bit heated. There was mention of Brandon Gaunt and of Helen Tudor, and whatever he said about her – Craig didn't catch it – made Geraint pretty angry. 'He was tamping' was how Craig put it. He didn't actually hear any direct reference to the autobiography this time, but he did hear Geraint say, 'I'll include anything I like that I know to be the truth and if you don't like it, well, I'll see you in court.' That was the point at which Lowe got up to go, but before he did, he said something that Craig found quite disturbing at the time, just before he strode back to his car."

"And what was it?" Fabia said impatiently.

"He said, 'You're an old man, Geraint, and you've already had a stroke. I could always arrange for you to have another one, there are ways and I'm more than capable of using them.'"

Fabia frowned. "Nasty, and I'm afraid he's right. There are several hard to detect poisons that can mimic a stroke or a heart attack, quite apart from anything else. You definitely need to have a word with this shit."

"I'm planning to, but Geraint wasn't poisoned."

"I know, but you told me he was drugged before he was pushed – if he was pushed?"

"I'm pretty sure he was, but I must have another word with Pat Curtis to clarify things." Matt leant his head back against the sofa cushions. "After seeing Craig, Dilys and I went and had a word with Geraint's sister and her husband, Glenda and Jon Armitage. They've got this plush restored farmhouse just outside Caerleon."

"What was she like?" Fabia asked. "Geraint told me they didn't get on."

"Well, she certainly didn't give the impression of being grief-stricken, that's for sure." Matt grimaced. "She came across as under extreme strain though. Dilys said she was sure she was frightened."

"But isn't that to be expected in the circumstances?"

"Yes, but I felt as if there was more to it than that. She certainly didn't hold back when it came to her feelings about her brother, and you would have thought she'd be careful what she said, but she wasn't. At one point she said she could have seen more of him, but she didn't want to. She was extremely tense, and the self-control could have slipped pretty easily if her husband hadn't been there. He's a smooth city gent type, and very much in charge. He kept a very close eye on her the whole time we were there. He said all the right conventional things about his brother-in-law but, there again, there was no emotion or warmth to it. But he was definitely more guarded than she was."

"And what about his financial problems? You said Sara had turned up some information."

"I asked him about that. He implied it was caused by a disgruntled employee they had to sack. We'll have to dig a bit deeper on that."

Matt rose and banked down the fire then turned and pulled Fabia to her feet. "But that's all for now, my darling. Time for us three to go to bed."

"This is the time that Thumper wakes up," Fabia complained.

"I know, but I'll rub your back, maybe that'll calm her down."

"Let's hope so."

Chapter 8

Matt had been in the office by half past seven on Tuesday to prepare for the press conference. It had gone smoothly enough, and he was impressed by the way Chief Superintendent Talbot handled it. She almost gave the impression she liked the press but, as she said to Matt afterwards, "They can be useful if you handle them right."

He'd wanted to say, 'I'll take your word for it, ma'am,' but he thought better of it. They were back in the office by ten o'clock and she told him she was meeting up with Fabia for a coffee. Matt was a little put out that Fabia hadn't told him this and his boss seemed to sense his reaction and explained that she'd had a meeting cancelled and taken the opportunity to call Fabia first thing.

Cassie Angel contacted them to say that the crowd of outside broadcast vans and other media gathered at the gates of Carreg Llwyd House had increased, and she was having trouble with knocks on the door every few minutes from people asking for interviews, strangers coming into the grounds and wandering around, and constant phone calls. Matt arranged for a block to be put on the phone line and for two more of his team to go to the house to control the paparazzi, but he knew there was no way he could get rid of them completely, much as he would have liked to.

Next had been a meeting with Pat Curtis who'd confirmed that there had been evidence of a barbiturate, probably Nembutal, in Geraint's body and that he had probably still been alive for a while after the fall.

"I believe he might have been inspecting some damage to the connection with the bricks, maybe leant out too far," Matt had suggested.

"But the fall wouldn't account for the injury to the back of his head," Dr Curtis had said. "He may well have been trying to sort out the balcony, if you can call it that, although I would have thought he'd have used a ladder. I asked Karen Johns and she agreed with me on that. No, he was definitely killed by a blow to the back of the head with something heavy, possibly metal. Given the shape of the wound it could have been a golf club, something like that. Not long before that he'd taken a dose of the stuff, so he might well have been feeling woozy when he was up there."

"The connection of the wrought iron to the brickwork was pretty dodgy before. Now it's virtually hanging loose," Matt told her. "I wouldn't have thought he was lifted over. He was a big man. It'd take someone very strong to do it."

"No, it wouldn't," she'd said briskly, her tone sounding as if she was talking to a rather dim-witted pupil. "I inspected the scene for myself. Those railings are low and there was bruising on the front of the torso as well. I think he must have fallen against them, then someone lifted him over and gravity did the rest. His injuries also indicated that he fell onto his back, but when he was found he was face down. I definitely think he was killed, well, finished off so to speak, after he hit the ground."

She turned as she got to the door. "Oh, and there was one other thing. He had some threads of yarn under the nails of his right hand. I've given them to forensics and they're examining them. I think they might be wool, but

I'm not sure of the colour yet. They might indicate that he grabbed at the clothing of whoever pushed him, or they might mean nothing at all. As to the rosemary sprigs in his hands, neither Karen nor I could make head nor tail of that."

Aidan Rogers was continuing his trawl through Geraint's computer, laptop and phone, while another officer was going through the records from the security cameras. Dilys had been reading through the manuscript of the autobiography while Sara Gupta had concentrated on Geraint's diary and correspondence. Becca Pryce, a young but enthusiastic detective constable who'd been working with Matt's CID team for a year now, had been set to research the backgrounds of the various people known to Geraint Denbigh – relatives, friends and possible enemies, with an emphasis on his work and private life away from Pontygwyn. Matt wondered if he was overloading her, but decided it'd be good training, and she seemed to have a methodical mind and an inclination to go above and beyond what was asked of her.

* * *

It was nearly lunch time when Fabia came back from having coffee with Erica Talbot. Although she'd asked Fabia a few questions about Geraint and the people he'd talked about, that hadn't been the main subject of their conversation. Erica said she'd wanted to use that as a pretext as she wanted to approach Fabia before she spoke to Matt. Now Fabia's mind was so full of what Erica had talked about that she hardly noticed the post scattered on the doormat and had to go back from the kitchen to pick it up. She wished she'd texted Matt and told him they were meeting up – she wasn't quite sure why she hadn't. Keeping things from each other was not a usual part of their relationship. Her mind in a daze, she only came to when the landline started ringing. Dumping her handbag on the kitchen table, she picked up the handset. "Hallo?"

"Is that Fabia Havard?" Although the slightly husky voice sounded familiar, Fabia couldn't quite place it.

"It is," Fabia replied, and waited, her curiosity piqued.

"This is Helen Tudor, I'm a friend of Geraint Denbigh's."

"Oh yes– I– er," Fabia stuttered, rather awestruck, then she pulled herself together. "Geraint talked about you a lot."

"Did he? Bless him, he was such a dear friend."

Fabia thought she detected a break in her voice.

"He told me about your aunt's letters and photographs. That was a sweet thing you did, giving them to him."

"Well, I suppose they were his, really, and I think Auntie Meg would have wanted him to have them."

"And now this awful news," Helen went on. "Mari, Geraint's niece, phoned me and told me that he'd been found dead, probably another stroke she said. I was only speaking to him a few days ago, and last time I was down this way I popped in to see him. He seemed perfectly fine then. I just can't believe he's gone."

"Nor can I, but I'm afraid it's all too true," Fabia told her. From what Helen Tudor had said, it sounded as if she was unaware that a murder inquiry was underway. Fabia wondered if she should mention it. She felt she had to. By tomorrow the news would have spread like wildfire across the papers, radio, television and social media. It was best she should hear from her rather than the media. "I'm afraid there was more to it than a stroke," she said.

"What do you mean?"

There was no gentle way to break the news. Fabia took a deep breath. "It wasn't a stroke. Geraint was killed, pushed over a balcony to the ground below."

"Oh my God! But who–? Why–? I don't believe it!"

"That's how I feel."

Down the line Fabia heard her take a deep, shuddering breath, then she said, "Look, I'm in Cardiff, staying with my cousin, can I come and see you?"

"Ah– of course," Fabia said, trying to keep the feeling of being star-struck out of her voice. Not an appropriate reaction in the circumstances, she told herself. Then it occurred to her that Matt would want to speak to Helen Tudor as well. "I'd better tell you – my partner, Matt Lambert, is the chief inspector in charge of the investigation."

"Is he?"

But she didn't probe any further and there was no way Fabia could tell if Helen Tudor thought this a good or a bad thing.

Fabia rushed on. "He might well need to talk to you. You might have information about Geraint's life that would be useful in finding the person who did this to him. Would you mind if I phoned Matt and asked him to be here? At least it would be better to talk to him here rather than at the station."

"Yes, I would prefer that."

The tone was a little sardonic and Fabia said quickly, "I didn't mean– well, I'm sure you know what I mean."

"Absolutely. Look, I can be with you in an hour, does that give you time to contact him?"

"It should do," said Fabia, crossing her fingers. Even if Matt wasn't available, she could always fix up another time for them to meet up, and she knew all about interviewing people in circumstances like these so she could do so herself. Fabia began to give Helen directions on how to get to Pontygwyn, but Helen said she knew it well and would be able to find her way easily enough.

For once Fabia managed to get through to Matt with no trouble and, once she'd told him about Helen's call, he said he'd be there. "I was planning to contact her anyway and this makes things easier. Anyway, thanks for... er..."

"I can't take the credit. It was her idea."

He didn't comment on this, just said, "Let me tell Dilys what's happening."

Fabia frowned. Matt's voice didn't sound right. She knew him so well and every nuance of tone was familiar to her. Maybe it was the stress of over-work, it often was. But this wasn't the time to ask.

Fabia could hear some of his exchange with Dilys in the background and was relieved when she heard Dilys say decisively, "I'm coming too, sir." If Matt was in a bad mood it would be easier if Dilys was there.

Matt came back to her. "Okay, we've just got a couple of things to tie up here and we'll be with you in about an hour."

Fabia simply said, "See you then," and cut off the call.

She pushed thoughts of what may be up with Matt to the back of her mind. There was no point in dwelling on it now. She decided to keep busy by getting the house tidied. It'd be best to use the sitting room rather than the kitchen, so she lit the fire in preparation, plumped up the cushions and tidied away several books and magazines, her laptop and some drawing materials, then had a quick dust of all the surfaces. Next she got out a tray, gave it a quick wipe and set out everything needed, changing her mind twice about what mugs to use. She grimaced as she thought how Matt would laugh if he could see her going to such lengths but, she told herself, it would be best to put Helen Tudor at her ease. If she had been as close to Geraint as it was rumoured, this news must be very difficult for her. What's more, she could be a valuable source of information. She could, of course, be a suspect too. No, Fabia thought, surely not.

Chapter 9

Helen arrived before Matt and Dilys. She was taller than Fabia expected, of a similar height to her. Her ash blond hair was gathered at the back of her head with a tortoiseshell clip and her make-up was immaculate. She studied Fabia for a moment with curiosity in her brown eyes, then smiled.

"You're just as Geraint described you," she said. "He told me you looked like your aunt."

"Did he?" Fabia said, pleased at the description. "Come in and sit down. It's cold out so I've got a fire going. Matt and his sergeant should be here any minute. Would you like some coffee, or tea perhaps?"

"Thank you, coffee would be lovely."

But before Fabia had the chance to show her into the sitting room, the front door opened and Matt and Dilys walked in. She studied his face carefully but, other than glancing at her briefly and away again, nothing showed her what was bothering him so, once again, she pushed it aside. She was bound to find out at some point.

Introductions were made then Fabia disappeared to the kitchen to make the coffee, and once they were settled, she waited for Matt to begin.

"Thank you for coming to talk to us, Ms Tudor," Matt said.

"Please, call me Helen."

Matt nodded in acknowledgement. "I hope you don't mind if I record our conversation. We would usually do so in these circumstances."

Helen frowned and, for a moment, Fabia thought she was going to protest, then she sighed and said, "I suppose so, if it'll help."

"It will," Matt said, and put his phone on the table between them. He tapped away at it, gave the date and the names of those present, and then sat back. "I'm sure you realise that the more information we can gather about Geraint Denbigh's background, particularly in the last few years, the more it will help us. Somewhere in that background will be the clues to why he was murdered and, hopefully, the identity of the murderer."

Helen winced at the word. "Are you sure it was murder?"

"Yes, I'm afraid so," Matt said. "At first, we thought it was an accident, but the pathologist has ruled that out." He paused. "Perhaps you could begin by telling me when you last had contact with Geraint."

"I suppose the most relevant conversation I had with him was a couple of weeks ago." She smiled briefly at Fabia. "That's when he told me about you and your aunt."

Fabia returned the smile but didn't comment. She didn't want to interrupt the flow. And Matt didn't say anything either, didn't even glance at her.

Helen took a deep breath, looking from one to the other with an expression which was a mixture of anxiety and sadness. "Geraint also told me that he'd been having some really unpleasant e-mails and phone calls. I told him to contact you – the police. He promised he would. Did he?"

"Yes," said Matt. "I spoke to him about ten days ago."

"Oh," she seemed surprised, and a little put out. "He didn't mention it to me, but then I've been busy rehearsing so he might have tried at some point."

"Or perhaps he found it difficult to talk about," Fabia said, unable to resist intervening. "Men sometimes don't want to admit they've been targeted. He may have thought talking to the police was somehow a sign of weakness."

Helen gave a rueful little smile. "That follows, knowing Geraint. Silly man." As she said this, Fabia noticed that her eyes filled with tears.

Without saying anything, Fabia pushed a box of tissues across the coffee table. Helen took one, dabbed at her eyes, then screwed the tissue up in her hand. She took a deep, shuddering breath, but before she could go on Matt steered the conversation into what he felt were more useful channels.

"Can you think of anyone who might have been responsible for the phone calls and e-mails?"

"Several people," she said. "Have you read through his manuscript yet? His autobiography, I mean."

"My sergeant, Dilys" – Matt turned to where Dilys sat – "has been going through the manuscript and she's highlighted several names. It's become obvious that some people would prefer the autobiography never saw the light of day."

"He doesn't hold back when it comes to those he disapproved of or who had let him down," Dilys said.

"I'm sure he didn't," Helen said. "He certainly had some scores to settle."

"Who with, exactly?" Matt asked. Although Matt had a pretty good idea, having read Dilys's notes, he wanted to know whether Helen would point out the same people.

Helen didn't respond immediately, just chewed at her lip and gazed across at Matt. Fabia was sure she was considering how much to tell him, as if she was sorting through a mental list, picking and choosing as she went.

"It's really important that we – Matt – should know who could have been a threat to him," Fabia said, once more unable to resist.

Matt flashed her a look of irritation. What was the matter with him? She sat back with a slightly apologetic smile.

Helen sighed. "I realise that it's important, but I don't want to drop anyone in it."

"You won't," Matt assured her. "We'll be very thorough with our investigation. We'll not make a move until we're absolutely sure of our information, which will be gleaned from several quarters, not just from you."

The silence in the room stretched out again. In the corner Auntie Meg's grandfather clock ticked away to itself, and from the kitchen there was a faint beeping, the dishwasher had finished its cycle. There was a whisper of pen on paper as Dilys sat taking notes, she always liked to jot down her impressions even if a recording was being made.

At last Helen responded. "There are several people who might have wished him harm," Helen said, and named a few.

Fabia felt the names she came up with were predictable, given information they already had.

"The director, Stephen Lowe," Helen went on, and Fabia noticed that as she said the words it was as if she had a very bad taste in her mouth. "Geraint gave him the sack when he was assistant director for one of his films because he was harassing some of the female actors. He's a nasty piece of work, completely amoral, and I'm sure he would have been very worried about what Geraint was writing. And the agent I mentioned, Brandon Gaunt, he's a sleazy bugger. He went in for that old-fashioned idea of the casting couch, got a couple of young female actors jobs they were completely unqualified for. Geraint and I were both pretty sure that they'd given in to Brandon's bribery. Geraint told me both these men had been to see him in the last few weeks urging him to be careful what he put into the autobiography, and both of them threatened him in one way or another." She took a deep breath then added, in a rush, "I'd say they're both capable of deciding to get rid of him."

Matt nodded but didn't mention that they were aware of the threats, just said, "We're planning to speak to them both."

"Good. I can give you their details, address and e-mail, etc., but I'd be grateful if you didn't tell either of them where you got the information."

"Don't worry," said Matt, "thank you for the offer, but I believe we've managed to get their addresses and other details."

"Good," she said, then took a deep breath. "And then there's Al Paver."

This was a name they weren't so familiar with. Fabia glanced at Matt, eyebrows raised, but he didn't react.

Dilys sat forward and said, "He's mentioned in the manuscript, but only briefly. Wasn't he married to Selina Spencer before she married Geraint?" she asked.

"Yes," Helen said, tight-lipped. "He's an absolute shit and I believe he was partly responsible for Selina's suicide. When she and Geraint split up, he started making trouble, and then he accused Geraint of pushing her into killing herself, probably trying to deflect attention from himself. Al and Selina had a daughter who must have been about ten at the time, a skinny little thing with a lazy eye."

"Do you think any of these men could have been responsible for the e-mails and phone calls?" Matt asked.

"Oh yes, I wouldn't be at all surprised."

"And is there anyone else you can think of who might have intended to harm him?"

Once again Helen sat in frowning silence, looking from Fabia to Matt and back again. Then Fabia noticed that her frown cleared, she'd obviously thought of something.

"Well, there are people nearer to home. His sister, Glenda, for instance. They were definitely not on good terms. He told me she'd accused him of deserting her, leaving her to cope with their father and being responsible for what she called 'the disaster', that was the loss of their land and status in the community. That sort of thing is very important to her. The thing is, most of that happened before Geraint left home, but he told me she still persisted in blaming him. It made me really angry, particularly as she's married to this mega rich bloke. They have three homes, would you believe?"

"So we've gathered," Matt said.

"You've spoken to them – her and her husband?"

"We have," Matt said, then changed the subject. "Is there anyone else you can think of who might have meant him harm?"

"No, not really, although he did mention that someone had plagiarised one of his projects, but he didn't tell me who. He said he was looking into it, but he hadn't decided what to do about it yet. He said it was awkward as there was more than one person involved and he didn't want to rock the boat. Unusual for Geraint, on the whole he enjoyed rocking boats."

"You have no idea who this person was?"

"Not really, though his niece, Mari, is in the same business so perhaps it was her." Helen frowned. "Although I doubt it, she was very fond of Geraint. I think she was closer to him than she was to her parents, well, her mother and stepfather. And he was fond of her as well, he used to talk about her a lot. Perhaps it was someone she knew, which could explain Geraint holding back on it."

"We'll look into that," Matt said. "In your opinion, would someone who'd done that go so far as to murder the person they'd stolen from?"

"No, not really," Helen told him. "I suppose it would depend on how much money would be involved should it come to court, and it's very unlikely that it would."

Fabia lifted a hand as if asking permission to speak, then quickly lowered it when Matt looked round at her. He gave her a nod and she went ahead.

"I believe plagiarism isn't in itself a criminal offence, unless there's also a copyright infringement. If there is, then any of the copyrighted material belongs to the writer or artist rather than the person using it."

Helen's eyebrows rose. "How do you know that?"

"I used to be in the police," Fabia told her, "but I'm now an artist, so I sort of know it from two different angles."

Helen smiled and said, "That's quite a change in career, you must tell me about it sometime."

Fabia got the impression she was relieved at the change of subject, but Matt wasn't about to let go yet. He sat forward, elbows on his knees. "Is there anything else you can think of that might help us?"

For a moment there was silence in the room. Helen looked down at her hands clasped in her lap, and Fabia could tell they were clasped tight. Matt waited for her to fill the void as Fabia knew he would.

At last Helen looked up and her eyes gave nothing away. "No, I don't think so. Of course, if I think of anything, I'll let you know immediately.

Matt was sure there was more, but he decided not to push it. He wanted her on side and not antagonistic.

"Well, thank you for your co-operation, and we'll let you know how things progress. Perhaps you could let us have your mobile number in case we need to contact you."

As she dictated it Fabia took the opportunity to key it into her phone as well, best to have it just in case.

Matt stood up and they all followed suit. Goodbyes were said and Fabia accompanied Helen to the door and watched as she walked down the path without looking back until she got to her car when she lifted a hand and, with a half-smile, got in and manoeuvred out of her parking space. Fabia turned back into the sitting room to see Matt putting his phone back into his pocket and Dilys closing her notebook.

"So, what did you think of that?" she asked.

"Useful," Matt said curtly, "although it didn't tell us much we didn't know already."

"I think there was more," said Dilys. "But she wasn't going to fess up; a bit of a closed book, she is."

"I think you're right," said Fabia. "Maybe I should keep in touch, she might come up with more if she doesn't think it's too official."

"I'd leave it to us, if I were you," Matt said.

Fabia shot him a glance, hurt and puzzled, and she noticed that Dilys looked a bit surprised. What was up with him?

"Ok-ay," she said carefully, but she couldn't resist adding, "Your boss did say I might be able to help, and in the past you've asked for my help, what's changed?"

"Nothing," Matt said. "Anyway, we must get going. I'll see you later, probably a lot later."

Fabia followed the two of them to the door. Dilys strode down the path as if wanting to escape, but before Matt could follow her Fabia grabbed his wrist. "What's up, Matt?"

"Nothing."

"Oh, don't give me that. You've been behaving like a grumpy bear ever since you and Dilys arrived. I know there's something on your mind and I think it's to do with me. Don't keep me in the dark."

He looked her in the eye at last. "There is something bothering me, but I haven't time to go through it now. I'll see you later. We can talk then."

"We'd better, Matt Lambert, because I'm not putting up with this atmosphere," she insisted. "And, by the way, the doctor says the backache is nothing to worry about and I'm fine, in case you're interested." And then she closed the door on him and leant against it, her hand on her stomach. That had been rather petty of her, but what the hell was going on?

* * *

As he drove back to the station Matt scowled out at the surrounding countryside. The weather suited his mood, glowering grey clouds threatened heavy rain and, as they came to the centre of Newport, large, penny-sized drops started to splash down on the windscreen.

Dilys, beside him, sat quietly. She hadn't commented on the interview with Helen Tudor or the fact that she could tell he was in a filthy mood. She knew him well enough to know that it was best to keep quiet in these circumstances. At some point she'd be sure to find out what was bugging him, and she was a patient body, willing to wait.

He parked and as they got out of the car Dilys said, "Shall I get Aidan to transfer the recording from your phone and sort out the evidence number, etc.?"

"Yes. Do that."

He handed the phone over to her then strode ahead into the station and up to his office. Dilys followed, frowning and a little worried. She hoped this mood wouldn't go on too long. She wondered if it had anything to do with the meeting he'd had with Chief Superintendent Talbot before the press conference that morning. What on earth could the chief have said to put him into such a mood? But there was no point speculating, she should concentrate on work. She went in search of Aidan.

Chapter 10

Mari stood at her desk holding the phone receiver, looking at it as if it could answer the turmoil of questions in her mind. She'd picked up the call as she'd rushed back into the empty office, everyone else had gone home. Now she subsided into the chair in front of her desk and sat there, fiddling with a pencil between finger and thumb, back and forth, back and forth, tap, tap, tap. She gazed at her computer screen but saw nothing.

The caller had been a friend of Tenniel's, Jason Kennedy, and what he'd told her had shocked her to the core.

"I've been away in the wilds of Brazil, got back yesterday," he'd told her, "so I didn't pick up on Tenniel's e-mail. He must have sent it all of three weeks ago."

Mari was used to Tenniel keeping in contact with Jason. He wasn't someone she had much time for, far too volatile and self-centred, but he and Tenniel had been friends since boyhood.

He'd rattled on. "I tried phoning his mobile, but he didn't pick up, so I decided to try the landline. I can't believe we're going to go ahead with the Lydia Phillips project. Talk about great news!"

"Lydia Phillips? What do you mean?"

Tenniel had told her they'd been discussing a project they might work on together, but he hadn't gone into detail, just that it was a drama, based in Wales, and the author was from the Valleys. He'd insisted he'd wait until he knew if it was going to take off, then surprise her. But this name rang bells. Mari frowned, trying to place it.

Jason didn't seem to have taken in her question, just talked over her. It was a habit he had. But what he said next had her sitting up and taking notice.

"I hadn't realised Tenniel was on such cosy terms with Geraint Denbigh, but I suppose his being your uncle it's understandable. What a gift! Good thing he's retired. I don't think he would have let go of that option if he was still working on it, far too hot! I mean, a coal mining village is such a brilliant setting, and the author is going to be up there with the greats in no time, especially after winning the Costa."

Then the penny had dropped, and Mari remembered. Geraint had mentioned this author; when was it? A while ago, she thought. He'd known the family way back and had been considering taking an option on the book Lydia Phillips had written, but then everything had been interrupted by his stroke. But Mari was sure he'd still been planning to go ahead at some point. And now Jason was talking as if Tenniel had the option. In the back of her mind suspicions began to take shape. She needed to find out more. Should she say anything about Geraint and the nightmare they were going through? No. She didn't want to put Jason off. Anger began to creep in. If what she suspected was true – oh God!

"I suppose so," she said now, surprised to hear her voice sounding more or less normal. "You think it could take off, do you?"

"Oh yes, a dead cert."

Mari winced at the word dead, felt her throat close up. If she'd tried to speak, no words would have come. But it didn't matter, Jason was in full flood.

"Tenniel told me he met up with her about six months ago at some bash in London. They got talking and hey presto! He said Geraint had gone cold on the idea and so he persuaded Lydia to sign up with him. I had my doubts about it at first, wondered if Tenniel had got the wrong end of the stick, but no, it was legit. I think he and Lydia became quite good friends over it, intimate friends if you know what I mean. Shit, the other phone's ringing. Ask Tenniel to get back to me, would you? Must go." And the line went dead.

Why had she sat there listening to him gabbling on? Hearing him talk of Geraint as if he was still alive had made her feel sick and words had stuck in her throat. Why hadn't she interrupted him? She tried phoning Jason back, but no luck, it went straight to voicemail.

Anger boiled inside her as the implications of what Jason had said gradually sunk in. How could Tenniel do this? There was no way her uncle would have passed on a good idea to him; he'd never made a secret of the fact that he thought Tenniel was a lightweight. "You're the one that keeps that company going, not him," he'd said on more than one occasion. She could hear the words echoing in her head. How could Tenniel have taken advantage of Geraint having a stroke? How could he take advantage of Lydia? Mari had met her and knew she was a rather unworldly and easily influenced person. She may be a very talented writer, but she certainly wasn't up to fighting her corner in a tough world. Had her agent or her publisher known about the relationship with Tenniel?

She threw the pencil she'd been fiddling with down and it bounced onto the floor. Ignoring it, she went and grabbed the office diary. They kept one for everyone to record appointments in, it meant each member of staff knew where the others were. Jason had said six months ago so she needed last year's diary. After a frantic search, she found it in the bottom of a filing cabinet and flattened it out on her desk. Flipping back the pages, she studied each entry and finally came to what she was looking for. 'HT dinner at Marco's. GD?' was scrawled across the page in Tenniel's untidy writing.

It was coming back to her now. It had been one of Geraint's rare trips up to London, he'd been there as Helen Tudor was receiving an award at the Critics Circle Television Awards ceremony. That was it! Tenniel had insisted that he should represent Cariad Productions since he was senior partner. Mari had been angry at the time as she'd wanted to be there, particularly as she knew her uncle would be going, but she'd given in as she often did when Tenniel dug his heels in. Tenniel hadn't told her they'd met up, but her uncle had. "Can't remember what we talked about," he'd said, "I'd had a skinful by then, mind. I should know better, must cut down."

Mari frowned and put her hand up to her mouth. Would Geraint have talked about an idea he was working on? The fact that he had been retired wouldn't have put him off tinkering with a good idea. Yes, it was possible. She had to get more information. Who to ask? Helen. Yes, she might know more. She rummaged in her handbag for her mobile and scrolled down to the number she wanted.

* * *

Restless and worried about Matt's moodiness, Fabia had decided to distract herself by going online to search for references to all the people involved in the case. She knew one of Matt's team would be doing exactly the same thing, but she wanted to do some of her own research. With Matt in such a foul mood, she doubted he'd take kindly to what he would see as interfering on her part, so she wouldn't tell him unless she came across something useful. Half the time he wanted her help, half the time he rejected it. She sighed. Distraction was what she needed.

She sat down at the kitchen table, opened her laptop and typed in the name Helen Tudor.

After half an hour of trawling through Facebook, Wikipedia, IMDb, and various media websites, the only useful things she'd come up with were references to Geraint and Helen's relationship, which had begun when he was directing a film she starred in in 2001. There were photos of them together at the premier and at various other events up until 2003, then a lurid account in one of the tabloids, with a blurred photo, of an argument they had in a restaurant, and various other bits and pieces of gossip about their break-up, all of which could have been fabricated by imaginative reporters desperate for a news story. But, thought Fabia, they could be based on truth, although she could find nothing that would indicate any reason for Helen to want to harm Geraint. Fabia was inclined to take the stories with a large pinch of salt. She'd suffered enough at the hands of the tabloids to know how far from the truth their coverage could be.

For the next hour she went through link after link, photo after photo, studying them all with her artist's eye, trying to get an idea from features and expressions what these people were like, but without animation and movement, it was hard to gather anything useful about them. She went through a few tabloid newspaper websites and found this a bit more useful, and her eyes widened as she came up with something interesting at last. Leaning forward, she studied the screen of her laptop, then searched for a magnifying glass and gave it deeper scrutiny. Yes, this could be useful. She considered phoning Matt, or maybe Dilys, to tell them what she'd found, but quickly decided against it. She'd wait till Matt got home.

* * *

Fabia was curled up on the sofa in the sitting room, dozing in front of the flickering television screen, hardly aware of a programme about building skyscrapers in some desert nation. The grandfather clock told her it was a quarter past ten. The fire was barely alight, and the room was cooling. She knew she should tamp the fire down, turn off the lights and get herself up to bed, but she just couldn't find the energy to do so.

"Come on, you stupid woman," she muttered and finally managed to haul herself upright. She collected an empty cup and plate – she'd taken to having cocoa and a snack before bed – and took them out to the kitchen. She was just about to mount the stairs when she heard Matt's key in the lock. She swung round, her hand on the newel post, and waited.

Matt didn't see her at first and while he was unaware of her presence, she had time to notice how tired he looked as he shrugged off his overcoat and hung it up. Her irritation from earlier in the day evaporated and she went to him and put her arms round his waist.

"My poor dear," she said. "You look absolutely knackered."

They stood there in silent mutual comfort for a moment, then Fabia leant back. "A hot drink? Wine? Something to eat?"

Matt pushed his hair back from his forehead. "Some of your *bara brith* and a glass of whisky, that would be perfect."

"Coming right up," Fabia said as he followed her into the kitchen.

Once she had placed a cut glass tumbler half full of his favourite Penderyn malt in front of him, together with slices of the rich fruit loaf, made to her Auntie Meg's recipe, she sat down at the kitchen table. Matt subsided opposite her and took a gulp of the whisky, then nearly choked as the heat of it hit his throat.

Fabia smiled. "Steady," she said.

She watched him for a moment as he chewed his way through his *bara brith*, trying to decide how to ask what was in her mind. In the end she decided to be upfront about it.

She was too weary to be tactful. "Are you going to tell me what was up with you this morning?" she asked.

"Ah, yes," Matt said. "The thing is... um... Chief Superintendent Talbot called me up to her office first thing this morning."

"Nothing unusual, I would have thought," said Fabia.

"No, and I thought she was going to ask for an update on the case, but it wasn't that at all."

"Then what was it?" Fabia thought she could guess.

Matt didn't give her a direct answer but said, "Have you heard of MASH, the Multi Agency Safeguarding Hub?"

"Of course. I helped set up the one in Newport."

"You did, didn't you? I'd forgotten that."

"So, what's that got to do with your grumpiness this morning?"

Matt gave her a rueful grin then pulled his hand down over his mouth. "Yea, well, I'm sorry about that, it's just that the chief took me by surprise, after all it's a bit off the wall, this idea of hers, and when we came to interview Helen Tudor I was still trying to process what she'd said, so–"

"Stop wittering, Matt, and get to the point." She reached over and clasped his hand to take the sting out of the words.

"She asked me if you would consider taking on a job."

Fabia made no comment.

"She says she wants to give the MASH personnel some further training, polish them up, as she put it, and she thought you'd be the one to do it. It'd only be part-time but you'd have a pretty free hand, and she wouldn't want you to start until later in the year, so after Thumper is born." Matt frowned across at her. "I said I thought it would be too much, what with the baby and all, but she pointed out that that was something you'd have to decide for yourself."

Eyes wide, Fabia didn't say anything for a moment, then she smiled. "She's a devious one, this new boss of yours. She runs it past you almost at the exact same time as she runs it past me but doesn't tell either of us she's going to. I said more or less the same to her, that I'd talk to you about it but ultimately it's my decision, and I also said I wasn't sure you'd be very keen on the idea."

Matt gave a sort of apologetic shrug but didn't say anything.

"Of course," she said, "you're right, I'll be very busy, and there's my painting and everything to take into consideration."

"Well, that's what I thought," Matt said, relaxing back in his chair.

She could tell Matt was relieved by her response and frowned. "Was this why you had a face like a wet week this morning?"

"I suppose so."

"But why did that idea put you in such a mood?"

"I was worried. If she, sort of, tempted you back into the force, even if it is in a civilian capacity, well, I'm not going to lie to you, I didn't think it'd be a good thing."

Fabia felt a little offended. "You don't think I could hack it?"

"No, no, that's not it," Matt protested, a little too vociferously, "but let's face it, it'd be quite a step down from when you were last in the force – superintendent to part-time associate. What if you came up against someone like Sharon Pugh? She'd most likely make things pretty difficult for you."

"I dare say I could handle it," Fabia said, her tone making it clear she thought she could make her own decisions.

"I know," Matt said, turning to her and taking her hand. "But I wouldn't want you to have to. And would it be a good idea for us to be working together?"

"We did before, Matt. I know it went a bit pear-shaped in the end, but this would be completely different.

Anyway, we wouldn't be likely to have much, if any contact with each other, would we?"

"You sound as if you're coming round to the idea."

Fabia could tell he wasn't pleased by the thought. She sighed, then pushed herself up from her chair. "Let's not talk about it now, Matt. I just want to get to bed and sleep, if the little monster will let me. Come on, time for some shut-eye."

But once in bed, listening to Matt's deep breathing beside her, she found she couldn't sleep as her mind went over and over Erica Talbot's proposal. Could she do it? Would it really be too much, as Matt suggested, or was it that he didn't want her encroaching on his territory? She'd been involved in several of his cases in the last few years and he hadn't made a fuss about it – well, not much of a fuss. But this would be more official. Was it that he wanted her to be the traditional mother, bound to the home and the baby? Surely not. No, that wouldn't be Matt at all. But as she tossed and turned, trying to get comfortable, she wondered whether, deep down, Matt felt that way. And with all that, she'd completely forgotten to tell him about the useful bit of information she'd found on her laptop.

Chapter 11

Mari was relieved to get through to Helen on Wednesday morning. She'd said nothing to Tenniel as she wanted to check on a few points before tackling him, and he was out of the office all day on Wednesday. She'd hardly slept for worrying about her suspicions, and the sound of Helen's deep honeyed voice saying, "Mari, my dear, how are you?" was somehow soothing.

"Not good, to be honest."

"It must be very difficult for you. I wish I could do more to help."

"That's kind, but there's not a lot we can do until the police release Geraint's body. Oh Helen, I can just hear him saying 'I could turn this into a damn good thriller', can't you?"

For a while they reminisced about Geraint, sharing memories, swapping ideas for the music and readings for the family funeral that would be held when his body was released. Inevitably there'd be a memorial service, probably in London, that would attract many from the world of theatre and film. But this wasn't what Mari had phoned for and she brought Helen back to what was most important at that moment.

"Helen, there was something I wanted to ask you. Do you remember getting that award from the Critics Circle?"

"I do, Geraint came up especially for it, bless him."

"And Tenniel was there too."

"Yes, he was. I'd forgotten that."

"Well, it's just that… it's difficult to explain, but did you see them together?"

There was silence on the other end of the line for a few moments, then Helen said, "I think I did, in the bar after the presentation. They looked as if they were in it for the long haul."

"Yes, that's sort of what Geraint said."

"Why do you ask?"

Mari didn't give her a direct answer. "Round about then, did Geraint mention an option he was taking out on a book?"

"He was always running ideas past me, but I don't remember anything in particular round then." There was a pause. "No, hang on a minute. I do remember something. He wanted to base a TV series in Wales, around the mining valleys, said it was about time after the success of *Gavin and Stacey*, but he wanted it to be something serious, more like those Scandi noir dramas. I think he'd found someone he was interested in."

"I thought as much," Mari muttered, more to herself than to Helen.

"You thought what?" asked Helen.

"Oh, never mind, it's just something… something to do with work."

"Come on, pet, you're worried about something, I can tell. It's hardly surprising at the moment I suppose. What is it exactly?"

Mari sighed. "There's nothing can be done about it, but what with Geraint and what's happened, I've been going over and over who might have done this awful thing, and, well I just wondered… no, never mind."

"You're not making sense, Mari darling." Mari could tell that Helen was smiling. "Come on, tell me what's on your mind."

Mari took a deep breath. Should she confide in Helen? She was sure it would go no further if she did, but it felt as if putting her fears into words would make them more likely to be true. And would it be a betrayal of her friendship with Tenniel? But if he had done what she suspected, wasn't that a betrayal of her, and Geraint? Before she could change her mind, she launched into a rapid account of the phone call from Jason Kennedy.

"So do you... do you see..." She stumbled to a halt and before she could go on Helen interrupted her.

"Let me get this clear, you mean to say that this project that Tenniel and this Jason person are so excited about is an idea they pinched off Geraint?"

"Yes, I suppose that is what I'm suggesting," Mari said slowly, still reluctant to admit it.

"Something like that came up when I was interviewed by the police and Fabia Havard. And you think Tenniel might be responsible for Geraint's death in order that all this doesn't come to light?"

"Yes, no, oh Helen, I don't know! The thing is, I don't think it's the first time he's done something like this."

"What? Pinched someone else's work?"

"Yes. Oh, I've been such a fool! Tenniel is always telling me I'm not tough enough for this business, maybe he's right." Mari could feel tears threatening and swallowed hard.

"I don't think being tough means you steal other people's ideas," Helen said briskly.

"I suppose not," Mari said. "Everything is so completely awful and weird at the moment. I just don't know what to believe."

"I have to say, it does seem a bit far-fetched, Mari, as a motive I mean," Helen said. "Maybe you should contact this Lydia Phillips person – the name's familiar somehow."

"Her first book won the Costa."

"Oh yes, I remember now." After a pause she added, "It might be a good idea to run it past Chief Inspector Lambert to begin with. He seems an approachable sort of chap, and he could speak to Lydia and see if she has anything useful to say."

But Mari wasn't at all sure she wanted to do that. By the time they ended the call Helen still hadn't convinced her it was the best thing to do.

* * *

"She's done what?" Dilys exclaimed as she stood by her desk, her mobile clamped to her ear.

Matt, who had been crossing the main office, looked round then went up to Dilys's desk.

"How many of them did you say?" Dilys glanced at him but said nothing while she waited for the person at the other end to answer her question. "I suppose it's hardly surprising," she said, "but we'll need to get it sorted. Enough is enough, especially if she's going to react like that."

There was another pause then Dilys said, "Okay, okay, we'll get some reinforcements to you now in a minute." She cut off the call.

"What's up?" Matt asked.

"It's that Cassie woman, sir. She's... well, it seems she's beaten up one of those paparazzi blokes."

Matt couldn't resist a grin. He hated the press crowd that gathered around a tragedy, called them vultures, in spite of the fact that Fabia always pointed out to him that they were only doing their job. Their hovering around waiting to pick up any titbit of news, sensational or not, took him back to a time he didn't want to remember when his sister, Bethan, had committed suicide by throwing herself off a bridge into the river Usk. But he mustn't think about that. He pushed the memories out of his mind.

"What exactly happened?"

"There's one hell of a crowd of them up at the house, sir. I suppose it's to be expected, and we've already sent a few PCs in uniform up there to keep an eye, and two of the specials, but I think we'll need more."

"But what about Cassie?"

"Apparently one of the paps got around into the back garden, near where Geraint was found, and was taking photos. Cassie saw him there and went apeshit. David Hywel says he heard this fracas and went round with one of the specials. They found this man streaming blood from a broken nose and Cassie standing over him with his camera – which she'd trashed – in her hand. They think she was about to hit him with it. They managed to calm her down and get her back into the house and took the photographer bloke to the van to clean him up. One of his mates is going to take him to the hospital to check on the damage, but it looks like we're going to have to go and check it over."

"It does, but I don't think we can stretch to any more personnel up there," Matt said, sounding exasperated. Then a gleam came into his eye. "But wait, I'm thinking in Charlie Rees-Jones terms."

"What's it got to do with our revered ex-chief?" Dilys asked.

"It's possible Chief Superintendent Talbot may be more understanding about deployment of staff. I'll go and have a word. You get up there, take Tom Watkins with you, and see if you can get rid of some of the vultures, or at least persuade them to keep their distance."

"Will do, sir. And, sir, I need to talk to you about the manuscript of his autobiography, I've made notes of a few more points that are worth pursuing."

"Good, we'll do that directly you get back."

Matt made his way through the crowded main office and up the stairs to the chief superintendent's office. He knocked on the door and when he heard a voice say, "Come," he went in.

He still found it strange to see the diminutive figure of Erica Talbot sitting behind the imposing desk instead of Charlie Rees-Jones's disagreeable bulk. Rees-Jones had been a thorn in Matt's flesh for many a year and his departure had been a great relief, not only to Matt but to many of his fellow officers. But he still hadn't got the measure, not entirely, of his new boss. She was a bit of an enigma. He couldn't imagine his previous boss ever suggesting re-employing Fabia, in fact the very thought made him want to laugh aloud.

She looked up as he came in and smiled. "Chief Inspector, what can I do for you?"

And that too was different, Rees-Jones would have growled at being disturbed and told Matt to get on with it, not to waste his time.

"It's this Denbigh case, ma'am," Matt said. "As you suggested, given his fame, the paparazzi have gathered outside the house in large numbers and it's getting a bit out of hand. His housekeeper, Cassie Angel, attacked one of them, destroyed the man's camera and did quite a lot of damage to his nose."

"Oh dear," the chief said, and he could have sworn she was trying not to smile. "Was she provoked?"

"Well, probably. Their very presence must be distressing for her, and this chap was sneaking round the back of the house, near to where Denbigh's body was found."

"Serves him right then, that's trespass."

"That's what I thought," Matt said, pleased that she agreed with him. "I've sent Sergeant Bevan out to check on things."

Given his height she was having to lean back to look at him. She flapped a hand and said, "Don't hover like that, Matt, sit down."

Once he had done so she said, "So why have you come to me?"

Matt leant forward. "Could we get a few more officers out there to keep order? It's a big property, but three should do it. I realise it's an extra expense and will take them away from other duties, but I think it's important to keep the peace out there until we can close the case and get rid of these people."

"Close the case? Are you anywhere near that?"

"No, ma'am, I'm afraid not, although I do have a couple of promising avenues to explore."

"Good. We really do need this cleared up as soon as possible. I've had the nationals, the BBC and Channel 4 News wanting the latest, although I've managed to hold them off so far. I think we'll have to speak to the press again at some point, sooner rather than later. Yes, you can have a couple more officers to control the crowd. Sort that out then get back to me about setting up another press conference."

"Thank you, ma'am, I'll get back to you soon as I can," Matt said, feeling relieved. However, this positive feeling didn't last long.

"While you're here, Matt, have you run my idea past Fabia?"

"I have. She... er... seemed interested."

"Good, good. I enjoyed meeting her, she's an interesting woman, we got on well."

She was smiling as she said this, and Matt was convinced she could tell he wasn't overly keen on the idea. What she said next confirmed this.

"I know you have doubts about it, Matt, but surely it's up to Fabia to agree, or not, as the case may be." There was a challenging glint in her eye as she added, "We women like to make our own decisions nowadays."

Matt clenched his teeth on a sharp answer. Was she suggesting that he would presume to make decisions on Fabia's behalf? That'd be the day!

There was an awkward little pause, then, "Of course, ma'am," he said.

She pushed herself up from her chair. "I must get on. I've a boring meeting with the mayor in half an hour."

Matt also got up and, after thanking the chief superintendent for her time, he made his way downstairs, feeling as if she had definitely got the better of him.

* * *

When he got back to his office there was no sign of Dilys. Matt glanced at his watch. It was ten past eleven. She'd still be up at Carreg Llwyd House sorting out the paparazzi. He looked forward to seeing her face when he told her they had been given permission to beef up the number of officers, and she'd have a good idea of who was best to send. Meanwhile he must reply to dozens of e-mails that had been piling up, but this had to be put aside when a call came through from an unexpected source.

When he picked up the phone the young constable on the switchboard told him, "There's an Inspector Singaram wanting to speak to you, sir, from City of London Police. Shall I put him through?"

Matt frowned. The name rang a bell. Oh yes, he'd met a David Singaram when he'd been on a course some years ago. Matt remembered that David had talked about his Mauritian parents, who had emigrated to the UK before he was born. They'd compared notes about living on small islands, since Matt's mother was from Guernsey, and they'd talked about the French connections that both islands had. They'd got on well and Matt had intended to keep in touch, but, as is so often the case, he'd not got around to doing so.

"Yes, I'll take the call," he said, and a minute later, "Hallo, David, how are you? It's been a long time."

"It has indeed, just over four years. I meant to keep in touch after that course, but there it is, life takes over."

"Same here," Matt said. "What can I do for you? You're still with the Serious Fraud Office are you?"

"I am, concentrating on financial fraud, to be precise."

"That's a tidy promotion."

"It certainly keeps me busy. And I gather you've made Chief Inspector. Congratulations."

"For my sins, yes, but what can I do for you?"

"I've been reading about this case you're working on, the Geraint Denbigh murder," David said.

"You have? So, what made you get in touch?"

"I saw in one of the tabloids, I think it was *The Mirror*, something about his sister being married to a financier called Jonathan Armitage."

"She is. Her name's Glenda. They've got a house near here, outside Caerleon."

"Small world. I'm on his tail for a potential fraud, working with HMRC, but I'm having to tread very carefully. He's got quite a high profile in financial circles and he also has a few friends in high places. I thought it might be useful to pick your brains, see if there's any connection. As you probably realise, I'm grasping at straws here."

"We did have some information come through about his company, Apudo Holdings, and I asked him about that. He was decidedly crisp in his answer, insisted it was just a disenchanted ex-employee stirring things up."

David gave a bark of laughter. "That disenchanted employee was one of his fellow directors, a Kenyan woman."

"Was she indeed? That puts a slightly different slant on things."

"He used to be with Transit Oil, and it looks as if he indulged in a spot of tax evasion while he was there. Would it be useful to you if I sent through the info I've got so far?"

"Definitely," Matt said. "If his brother-in-law had turned up information on his activities, should they be criminal, I'm sure he wouldn't have wanted them broadcast. His wife did not get on with her brother and, what's more, Denbigh was writing his autobiography; it's a bit of a tell-all, truth-will-out exercise so far as we can see."

"Have you had sight of the manuscript?"

"One of my staff is trawling through it but there's been no mention of Armitage yet, though I doubt he would have known that. He could well think that Denbigh had put in incriminating information. It'd be useful to us if he had." Matt pushed his untidy hair back from his forehead. "Of course, he could have believed that Denbigh had information of that sort about him anyway, autobiography or no autobiography. Either could give him a motive."

"True," said David, "although I wouldn't have thought that someone who worked in the film industry would have much of a clue about financial shenanigans."

"I don't know so much, what about having to get funding for their film and television projects? Wouldn't you have to have some knowledge of how things work in the financial world? What are those backers called who pour money into theatre? Angels, isn't it?"

"Yes, you have a point. Anyway, I'll keep you posted," David said, then changed the subject. "So, how's life with you? I seem to remember your boss had a few problems when we last saw each other, what was her name? Fabia something. I remember that."

Matt took a deep breath, not sure whether he wanted to go over the events of the last few years with someone he hardly knew, but David was doing him a favour, so he supposed he ought to give him some kind of answer. "Fabia Havard, yes, she was accused of corruption, but we managed to clear her name, although she didn't go back into the force."

"Well, that's good news, clearing her name I mean. I got the impression the two of you were quite close."

"You could say that," Matt said, smiling.

"Sounds to me as if there's more to the story than you're letting on," David suggested.

"There is, I suppose." As briefly as he could, Matt told him that he and Fabia were now living together. "Fabia's expecting, the baby's due in a few weeks' time."

"Congratulations, mate. That's quite a story. My three are grown up now, well, teenagers. Enjoy the baby while you can, they grow up far too quickly."

As Matt ended the call, he could hear Dilys in the main office and got up to go and tell her about the information that would be coming through. He also wanted to let her know that they'd been given permission to co-opt more officers. But he didn't get the chance to tell her about any of it.

Chapter 12

Once again, Dilys was standing at her desk, the phone receiver clasped to her ear, sounding exasperated. "You'll just have to tell him that the chief inspector is busy. He can't just pitch up and expect to be treated like a— like bloody royalty." When she saw Matt she said, "Hang on, Karim," and put her hand over the receiver. "It's Karim Singh on reception, sir. They've got that Stephen Lowe down there demanding to see you, one of those 'do you realise who I am?' types, looks like. He says he's going to sit there until you agree to speak to him."

"I was going to have to interview him, anyway, so now is as good a time as any. Tell Karim to say I'll be there in a minute, then I'll give it twenty minutes or so before going down. Let him wait a bit."

Dilys grinned and turned back to the phone. "The chief inspector will be down in a bit. Let him cool his heels," she said.

"Ask them to put him in one of the interview rooms, number three preferably, it's gloomier than the rest, it'll give him a taste of reality," Matt said. "You'd better come too, Dilys, and can you get me a transcript of that interview with Craig Evans? The part where he mentions Stephen Lowe and Geraint having a row."

"Will do, sir."

"But before you do that," Matt said, "did you manage to calm things down at Carreg Llwyd House?"

"Just about. Cassie is one angry woman. I swear I could see steam coming out of her ears!"

"When it comes to the paparazzi, I'm with her all the way."

Dilys gave a little nod, she knew the history and sympathised with her boss. "Anyway," she said, "I managed to calm her down, and I do feel sorry for her, but I pointed out that hitting out like that wasn't going to solve any problems. The bloke she thumped isn't going to press charges, not since I told him he was trespassing and could be prosecuted. I gave the crowd of them a little pep talk, you know, have sympathy for the family – Cassie, that is – and keep their distance. I hope it works."

"And the chief says we can deploy a few more up at the house, so that should help."

"Good. Well done, sir," Dilys said, giving him a cheeky grin.

Matt responded with a slightly grim smile but didn't comment.

"Before we go down to talk to this bloke, does he feature in the autobiography at all?"

"Not significantly. He is mentioned… what was it Geraint called him? A minor director of dubious talents. And he mentions having to sack him at one time because he was touching up the female members of the cast and they were complaining. That comes across as something Geraint Denbigh thoroughly disapproved of."

"Good, that'll do for now."

* * *

Half an hour later he and Dilys made their way down to an interview room on the ground floor. It wasn't as bleak as the interrogation rooms, but it certainly wasn't homely. There was a small, highly placed window which looked out on to an alleyway to the side of the station, making the room rather dark, but the ceiling light had been turned on. The walls were painted a dull grey-blue and were bare except for a large map of the Newport area and a framed photograph of the Steel Wave. A table jutted out from the wall opposite with recording equipment at one end, and there were padded office chairs, one on one side and two on the other.

A short, tanned man wearing what Dilys could tell was a very expensive suit was pacing up and down the room. He turned and glared at them, running an impatient hand over his sleek, dark hair as he did so.

"About time," he snapped. "I haven't got all day."

"Good morning, sir, my apologies for keeping you waiting," Matt said calmly. "Please take a seat." He indicated the chair on the far side of the table and he and Dilys sat down opposite him. "I am Chief Detective Inspector Lambert, this is Detective Sergeant Bevan. We will be recording this interview," he said as Dilys began to set up the equipment and recorded the date and those present.

Stephen Lowe ignored Dilys but said to Matt with a stretch of his lips that was more sneer than smile, "Going to put me through the third degree, are you? Hardly seems appropriate when I've come here of my own free will to help you."

"Not at all, sir. As you say, you have come here voluntarily so you are free to leave at any time," said Matt. "The recording is standard procedure. Perhaps you could give us your full name and address."

"If I must. My name is Stephen George Lowe, you've probably heard of me," he said, his eyebrows raised as a condescending smile played at his lips.

Neither Matt nor Dilys made any comment and, after an awkward silence, he shrugged and gave them an address in North London. "But while I'm in Cardiff, I'm staying at the Coldra Court Hotel."

Matt sat forward in his chair. "Could you give us your reasons for asking to speak to us?"

"I heard about Geraint Denbigh's death, an absolute tragedy, very upsetting. And now I hear that it's thought it wasn't another stroke, that... er... foul play is suspected." He looked at Matt, eyebrows raised in query.

"Yes, that is the case," Matt said without further explanation.

"I caught the tail end of a press conference you gave yesterday. Am I right in thinking you are in charge of the investigation into his death?"

"I am, and my team," Matt said, with a nod towards Dilys.

"Well," he said, sitting back and folding his arms across his chest, "since I am... was a friend and associate of his, I thought it was my duty to offer you my help."

"That's very public-spirited of you, sir," Matt said.

"I do my best," Lowe said smoothly.

"Can you tell me when you last saw Geraint Denbigh?" Matt asked.

"It must have been about a month ago. I was in Cardiff on business, as I am now, and I decided to drop in on him as I had a bit of time on my hands."

"And would you say you were a close friend of his?"

"Yes, I would. We worked together on several productions."

"And he was pleased to see you?" Dilys asked, deciding it was time to make her presence felt and remembering what Helen Tudor had said about Lowe.

His reaction was predictable. He didn't even acknowledge her but answered as if Matt had asked the question. "I believe so," he said. "It's always good to meet up with old friends."

Matt was puzzled. He couldn't work out why this man had made a point of coming to speak to them. Did he have

106

anything valuable to tell them? Why had he appeared at the station with no warning? Did he realise he could be a suspect?

"So," Matt said slowly, "the two of you were on good terms?"

"I would say so, yes."

Matt hadn't got time to waste so he decided to cut to the chase. Dilys had laid a small pile of paperwork on the table in front of them and now he pulled it forwards and leafed slowly through the pages. Having found the one he wanted, he looked up at Lowe who was sitting with one hand on the table in front of him, apparently relaxed except for his fingers tapping at the surface.

"That is not the impression we have, Mr Lowe." He glanced down at the piece of paper before him. "We have a record here of what is probably your last visit to Geraint Denbigh. Of course, there may have been others after this one which was" – Matt glanced at the piece of paper in front of him – "exactly a week before he was killed."

Stephen Lowe showed little sign that he'd understood the implications of what Matt had said, except for the fact that his eyes narrowed a little. But he remained sitting back in his chair and let his hand drop to his lap.

"I think that's the last time I saw him," he said. He didn't ask them how they knew but simply waited for Matt to go on.

Matt glanced at Dilys, pushed the piece of paper towards her and indicated one point on the page. Dilys looked at it and nodded.

Lowe looked from one to the other of them, not quite as cool now. He frowned and said, "What's all this about? I think you should tell me what you're playing at."

"Playing at?" Matt said. "I'm definitely not playing, sir. We have a witness to what you say is your last visit to Geraint Denbigh."

"Witness? What do you mean witness? There was nobody else there. He said his housekeeper was out."

"She was, but there was a gardener at the house. I believe he went to find Geraint and you followed him round to the back of the house."

"Oh yes, of course. I'd forgotten."

"Well, this young gardener, overheard your conversation with Geraint and his account of it is not of an exchange between friends, far from it. In fact, he says you threatened Geraint."

Lowe said nothing, just scowled across at Matt, who glanced at the piece of paper again then continued. "He heard Geraint state that he'd include anything he liked in his autobiography and that if you didn't like it, he'd see you in court. Is that correct?"

There was no response, so Matt went on. "He also told us that you threatened Geraint. You pointed out that he'd had one stroke and you could arrange for him to have another one. Is that true?"

Lowe put up a hand and dragged it down over his mouth, gazing at Matt speculatively over his fingers. What he'd been told hadn't dented his self-assurance nearly as much as Matt had hoped it would. Matt wondered what was going on, but he said nothing. Both he and Dilys waited, in silence, for him to respond. When he did, it seemed he'd decided to go on the attack and bluff it out.

"And you'd take the word of a scruffy young gardener rather than mine, would you?"

"That depends entirely on what you have to tell me," Matt said.

"Geraint and I did have a bit of a difference of opinion, but nothing as colourful or dramatic as this gardener chappie implies. We also discussed some others who may not be too happy about the publication of his autobiography. You've heard of an actress called Helen Tudor I suppose?" He didn't wait for Matt to respond. "Anyway, she and Geraint were an item some time ago and their affair ended rather messily. Then there's a chap called Brandon Gaunt, an agent; he and Geraint had a few run-ins at one time. And, of course, there's Al Paver who used to be married to Geraint's ex-wife, before he was, that is. Now that would be a man you should interview. As to me…"

He paused and Matt had a strong suspicion that they were about to get to the real reason for his being here. Matt waited, as did Dilys, sitting quite still and attentive beside him.

Lowe leant forward, his elbows on the table, his hands clasped. "But you're not going to fit me up with a murder charge, Chief Inspector, as I was out of the country when Geraint was killed, and I can prove it."

Matt was irritated by the man's attitude. He felt as if he was playing some game and wasn't telling them the rules, but none of this showed when he simply said, "Perhaps you'd like to elaborate."

"Am I right in thinking that Geraint died last week?" he asked, his face serious now.

"Yes, last Friday," Matt told him.

"There, you see," he didn't bother to keep the triumph out of his voice. "I was in France, Saint-Malo to be precise, staying at the Hotel De Gersigny. They'll confirm I did so, and I was working with a French film producer on a project we're both involved in which will be filmed over there. His name is Théo Renier and I can give you his address so that you can check I'm telling the truth." With this he sat back in his chair and crossed his arms, giving Matt a smug little smile.

Silence reigned for a few moments then Matt said, "Thank you, sir. Perhaps you would be so kind as to jot down Monsieur Renier's contact details for us."

Matt pushed a piece of paper over the table, together with a pen, and Lowe wrote them down with a flourish then slid the paper back across to Matt. When he'd done that, he pushed his chair away from the table. "Is there anything else I can do for you, Chief Inspector? I do have a meeting" – he glanced at his wristwatch – "in half an hour."

Matt turned to Dilys. "Are there any questions you'd like to ask Mr Lowe?" he said.

Dilys took the hint and said, "Yes, sir. Mr Lowe, you mentioned Helen Tudor, can you tell us why you think she would wish to harm Mr Denbigh?"

This time he directed his answer at Dilys. "What is it some writer said? Shakespeare, I think it was him. Hell hath no fury like a woman scorned."

"You believe that Geraint Denbigh ended their relationship," asked Dilys calmly, "and she could be after revenge for that rejection?"

Lowe shrugged. "It's always possible."

"But you don't know for sure?" Dilys pressed him.

"No, I don't know for sure, as you so charmingly put it, but I do think it's worth some attention from your chief. Perhaps he'll be more detached about it."

You really are a very silly man, Dilys thought. "And one more thing," she said. "Am I right in thinking that you and Geraint fell out when working together some years ago, he objected to your treatment of the female members of the cast of the film you were working on?"

Lowe pulled at his bottom lip. He was now looking straight at Dilys. "And where did you get that idea from?"

Dilys glanced at Matt who gave her a small nod. "I read about it in the manuscript of Geraint Denbigh's autobiography. All in all, it's been very informative."

"But definitely only Geraint's take on things," Lowe said scornfully. "Yes, he did give me the push, but I think it was more because said female cast members preferred to spend time with me rather than him. He liked his women to gather round, worshipping at the feet of the great man. I think that's why he asked me to leave, because he wasn't getting the usual amount of female attention. I could have made a fuss, but I was fed up with dancing to his tune. So I left."

"I see, sir," said Dilys, allowing her doubts about this account to show in her voice. "Thank you, Mr Lowe." She turned to Matt. "That's all I have to ask, sir."

"And what about the two men you mentioned, Brandon Gaunt and Al Paver?" Matt asked.

Lowe seemed to relax now that the questions were coming from Matt. "I just think they're worth your attention," he said, "given that both of them fell out with Geraint in quite spectacular ways. Much worse than I did. With Gaunt because Geraint objected to his behaviour towards women, yet again. He was such a puritan."

This seemed to contradict what he'd told Dilys, but Matt let it go.

"And with Paver," Lowe added, "because he hated the fact that Geraint had stolen – Paver's words – his wife from him. Of course, she committed suicide a few years later and he stirred things up over that as well. Paver, by the way, is in London at the moment, staying at The Strand Palace Hotel. He phoned me a couple of days ago, wanted to meet up, but I told him I wasn't available. He's not the kind of person I want to waste my time on. Anyway, it'd be worth your while having a word while he's in the UK. And now I must get going. I hope I've helped with your investigations. That was my intention."

Like hell it was, Matt thought. "I'll see you out," he said.

Chapter 13

"When it comes to a blatant attempt to establish an alibi, that took some prizes!" Matt said to Dilys when they were back in his office. "We'll need to check the Hotel de Gersigny, and I'll get on to Jacques Hubert at the Commissariat Central in Saint-Malo, ask him to do some digging. He's a good bloke, we used to go fishing together when the family went to France on holiday."

Dilys didn't often get the chance to ask about Matt's past so she risked taking the opportunity now. "When was that, sir?" she asked.

"When I was a teenager. We'd go to my mother's family in Guernsey for a week then to France for a few days, we stayed in a *pension*, a sort of B&B, owned by his parents. Jacques went into the French force about the same time I joined up."

Dilys laughed. "Is there any force where you don't have contacts, sir?"

"Plenty," Matt said, grinning. "But where I don't have any, Fabia probably has."

"Quite a team."

"You could say that," he said, but Dilys noticed the grin fade rather quickly.

She wondered why but didn't ask and decided to change the subject.

"As to that Al Paver bloke, do you want me to check up on him?"

"Yes, do that would you?"

"Will do," Dilys said, turning to go, but then she turned back. "I've all but finished reading through the manuscript. Have you got a moment now to go through the notes I've made?"

"Absolutely," Matt said. "Bring it in."

Dilys was back with her laptop within moments. She put it down on Matt's desk and drew up a chair. Matt sat down beside her, and she opened up the laptop and made her way to the file she wanted.

"These are the notes I've made," she told Matt. "They're in chronological order so not exactly in order of importance as I see it, I hope that's okay."

"I trust your judgement, Dilys. Right, who's first?"

"I've gone right back to when he left Wales and moved to London. He did various jobs as a runner in production companies and theatres, they do all the donkey work, and he did that for two to three years basically learning his trade and writing in his spare time. He sent off several scripts and got lucky with his fourth. According to him that's pretty quick, but he'd been doing a lot of networking, it seems. This play was picked up by a very rich American woman who owned and ran a theatre in North London" – Dilys leant forward to read the name – "The White Dragon Theatre, it was called."

"Pity it wasn't the Red Dragon," Matt said.

"Yes, but maybe just the dragon bit was a sign of good luck for him, a tidy connection to home. Anyway," Dilys continued, "her name was Beverley Drake and they got married in 1967, which was about the time his career took off. According to Geraint he was her toy boy, since she was fifteen years older than him, but it sounds as if it was a happy marriage. They moved to New York, but she was killed in a car crash in 1979. He seems to have been really cut up." Dilys paused. "Sorry, sir, all that isn't exactly relevant to the case, but I really got into his autobiography, it's fascinating. It seems he inherited a fortune from his wife and that enabled him to spread his wings a bit. Right. Where am I?" Dilys ran the cursor up and down her notes then stopped. "In 1985 he had a play going strong on Broadway and one of the actors was Selina Spencer. To cut the story short, they got married within three months of meeting, but it was rocky right from the start. He says in the manuscript that he was in lust rather than in love with her. Apparently, she was quite a looker. But it seems he had a good relationship with her daughter, Rose, who was four at the time they got married, but both the kid's birth father, that's Al Paver, and Selina herself seemed jealous of the fact he was close to the daughter."

"What happened to the kid?"

"During the four years of their marriage, Selina had a drink problem and also suffered from bouts of depression, and Geraint was working all hours that God gave, travelling backwards and forwards between New York and London, so the child spent more time with Paver than with them. At one point Geraint says that he regretted this as he'd enjoyed looking after her and used to read her Welsh fairy stories and stuff, but he didn't feel he could make a fuss about it. By the time the marriage ended, which was in 1989, he was hardly seeing her at all."

"So, after the divorce, did he see any more of his wife and Paver?" asked Matt.

"Some. It was a messy divorce. Selina accused him of abuse, which he denied, but Paver got involved and it all went to court. Geraint was cleared, mainly because the kid's nanny spoke up on his behalf, but things came unstuck again when Selina committed suicide and Paver blamed him. That was the point at which he came back to live in London permanently."

Matt sat back and ran a hand through his untidy hair and frowned. "Is there anything in there about Paver that might give him a reason to want to get rid of Geraint?"

Once more Dilys ran her finger over the touchpad, searching for the notes she wanted. "Here we are," she said. "Look at that note I've made by there."

Matt leant forward and read from the screen.

> Paver was a property dealer. According to GB he was deep into diddling the revenue by playing around with the complicated tax systems in New York. GB says he could have reported several deals to the police which would have got Paver into trouble, but he didn't for the sake of Rose as he felt she'd had enough to cope with.

"He does say that he still has access to all the evidence that'd be needed to prosecute Paver – how did he put it? 'For my own protection.'"

"I wonder what he meant by that?" Matt said. "We'll have to do some more searching through his paperwork and computers with that in mind."

"I'll see to that," Dilys said and jotted down a reminder in the notebook that went everywhere with her.

"Okay, so what else have we got?" Matt asked.

"Throughout the manuscript there's mention of his relationship, or lack of it, with his sister. She used to write to him regularly when he first left Wales asking for money, begging him to come back, complaining about having to look after their father, who seems to have been quite a handful. One of the reasons Geraint went to London is that he was ordered out of the family home by their father. Geraint accused him of drinking away their inheritance, and it seems he sold off a hell of a lot of their land even before Geraint left home. It's very sad, really. In the end his sister stopped contacting him, round about the time she got married to a local doctor, that's Mari Reynolds' father. They divorced ten years later, and Glenda married her present husband who's loaded, at least he is as far as we know – very much the high-flying city gent."

"But, as we know, also suspected of some shady practices." Matt's tone was sardonic.

"Yes, and there's quite a lot about that as well."

"Is there anything about his relationship with Helen Tudor?" Matt asked.

"Yes. They got together when they were both working on the same film, it was his script and she was female lead, but it didn't last very long. He says that work got in the way. He was in London, she was in New York, or vice versa, but they agreed to part quite amicably and have remained friends."

"So, it's the same men that we already have in the frame, Lowe, Gaunt and Paver, I suppose. Then there's Armitage, with his sister as a possibility, and Helen Tudor I suppose, but I doubt that very much. Then there's person or persons unknown." Matt sat back and sighed. "Not much to go on, but I do have an idea that's been niggling at me for a couple of days. Meanwhile I'd better have a look at the info that David Singaram sent through, see if there's anything there to hang a hat on. The other thing I'd like a look at is his will. Do we know who his solicitor is?"

"Yes. Sara turned up some correspondence with John Meredith of Granger, Meredith & Llewellyn in Hendre Avenue. You know him, don't you?"

"I do indeed," Matt said, sounding pleased. "Don't you remember he married Anjali Kishto, the Mauritian designer? She was involved in that awful business when Caradoc Mansell was murdered."

"Oh yes, White Monk Abbey."

"That's it." Matt smiled and pushed himself out of his chair. "Right, Dilys, thank you for all that. My next job, I think, is to contact John and see if I can get a look at the will. I'd like to know *cui bono*."

"If you're trying to catch me out, sir, no luck," said Dilys with a grin. "That means who benefits."

Matt laughed. "Can't get one over on you, can I? Won't stop me trying, though."

* * *

Matt had got through to John Meredith more quickly than he'd anticipated and, at half past four that afternoon, he parked his car in Hendre Avenue. As he walked along to the three-storey town house, which, like so many nowadays, was more likely to contain offices than a family, he looked over to the opposite side of the road where an old chapel had been converted into an art gallery. Matt remembered that Fabia had had an exhibition there a few years ago. So much had changed since then.

He strode up the steps and pushed open the front door, beside which was a shiny brass plaque announcing 'Granger, Meredith & Llewellyn, Solicitors and Notary Public' and the same in Welsh below this. A door to his right led him into a reception area where a young man sat behind a desk.

"Can I help you?" he asked Matt, then he smiled. "Ah yes, Chief Inspector Lambert, isn't it?"

"Yes, and you're Stephen Powell, John's assistant, aren't you?"

The man nodded. "He's expecting you. Have a seat, Chief Inspector, and I'll go and tell him you're here."

Matt wandered across to look at a couple of paintings on the wall and realised one of them, a watercolour of a sunset over Gwiddon Park in Pontygwyn, was by Fabia. He smiled as he remembered her telling him that John had bought it when she had the exhibition.

He didn't have to wait long before John appeared. He was a slight, sandy-haired man with intelligent blue eyes. He held his hand out to shake Matt's.

"Good to see you, Matt, how's Fabia?"

"Looking forward to when the baby's born, she says she feels like a whale."

John laughed. "Anjali said something similar when Lisa was on the way."

"How are they both?" Matt asked as he followed John into his office.

"Well. Anjali's designs have really taken off, so much so that we've had to employ a childminder, but Lisa loves going there. She's nine months going on thirty, that child, already nattering away; some words are actually recognisable. When is your little one due?"

"Just four weeks to go now."

"Good Lord. The time seems to have flashed past, but I doubt that's how it seems to Fabia."

"You could say that," Matt said, with a rueful grin. "The thought of being a father is pretty daunting isn't it?"

"It is, but take it from me, it's the most joyous, and exhausting, thing that could happen to anyone."

"It's the exhausting bit that Fabia and I have been thinking about."

"That won't last," John said breezily. "Anyway, have a seat." John settled himself behind his desk and leant forward with his arms crossed. "Well, what can I do for you?"

"I suppose you've heard about Geraint Denbigh's death?"

"Yes, I heard from his sister, Glenda Armitage. She wanted to know what was in the will. Actually, I was going to—"

"Ah," said Matt. "Did you tell her?"

"I did. Since I'm his executor I thought it was okay to give her a brief outline, but that was before I saw your press conference yesterday. Are you sure he was murdered?"

"I'm afraid so, and there are definitely people around who would have liked to see the back of Geraint Denbigh.

He was writing a tell-it-all type of autobiography and pointing the finger at quite a few people, quite apart from the fact that he and his family, well, his sister, had fallen out. It's a bit of a job trying to sort the wheat from the chaff."

"I'm sure you'll get there in the end, Matt. You usually do. Is Fabia involved this time?"

Matt grimaced. "Would you believe her Auntie Meg, the one who left her the house, was an old flame of Geraint's? You couldn't make it up, could you?"

John gave him a wide-eyed but rueful grin. "No, you couldn't, but I did know that, actually. Geraint mentioned it the last time I saw him."

"They'd got quite close." Matt grimaced. "She's pretty cut up about his death."

"I'm sure she is," John said sympathetically. "And it's yet another murder for her to contend with. Poor Fabia, not the best thing to happen when she's so near giving birth. I guess her emotions are pretty near the surface, if you know what I mean."

"Yes, but she's determined to become involved." Matt sighed. "But then she usually comes up with the goods, so I shouldn't complain. Enough of that, what about this will? Can you give me the bare bones?"

"Well, the first thing I have to tell you," John said, with a smile, "is that he's left Fabia something in his will."

"What?" Matt said, eyes wide in surprise.

"I'll get Stephen to bring in a copy, and some coffee as well. Let's sit over there." John indicated a couple of easy chairs on the other side of his office. "It'll be more comfortable."

Five minutes later John was sorting through the papers that Stephen had brought in for them along with a tray holding two steaming mugs of coffee and a bowl of sugar.

"This is a copy," John said, handing Matt a couple of sheets of papers. "If you want to make notes on it, feel free. The bit about the ring is a codicil that he signed when he came in. He's left Fabia his signet ring because Fabia's aunt gave it to him just before he left Wales."

"Oh, I see," Matt said, and silence reigned as he read through the documents while John sat back and sipped at his coffee.

Occasionally Matt made a note, underlined a sentence or highlighted something with a marker pen he'd rummaged for in his pocket. At last he sat back, noticed his cooling coffee, took a gulp of it, then looked across at John.

"As to the rest, as I understand it, he leaves the house and all its contents to his niece, Mari. Then he leaves a hefty chunk of money to his sister, Glenda Armitage, which surprises me since they seemed to be at loggerheads." He picked the paper up again and glanced down it. "Then there's a generous bequest to Helen Tudor, and he's left her the manuscript and all his researches for the book too, he says that is in case he doesn't live long enough to finish it. He asks that she should do so and get it published. There's another bequest to the Actors' Benevolent Fund, and a smaller but substantial one to Cassie Angel. After that a few odds and ends to friends he names but I haven't heard of any of them, I hope you have," he said, giving John a rueful smile. "Then we come to the last one: 'to Rosemary Caroline Spencer, daughter of my ex-wife, Selina Spencer, my collection of books of Welsh fairy tales, legends and folklore because she loved them when she was four years old'. She had her mother's surname rather than her father's, it seems."

"Who was her father?"

"Selina was married to Al Paver, a New York property developer of dubious reputation. They divorced before she met Geraint, but Paver seems to have gone on having contact with her and their daughter. Selina committed suicide six months after she and Geraint broke up and the kid had gone to live with her father by then. Paver accused Geraint of being the cause of her suicide." A thought occurred to Matt. "Do you think his sister and her husband, and his niece, knew about these bequests?"

John shook his head. "I'm pretty sure they didn't because, when he came to my office to talk about drawing this will up – as you see it's a recent one, signed and witnessed just three months ago – he told me his family would be surprised by its terms and he wished he could be around to see their faces. That indicates to me that he didn't expect them to know about it until after his death."

"It does, doesn't it. Reminds me of that business with Caradoc Mansell."

"The thought had occurred to me," John said.

Matt pushed himself up out of the comfortable armchair. "I must get back to the station. Can I take this copy with me? And can I tell Fabia about the signet ring?"

"Of course, to both," John said, smiling as he rose to show Matt out. "I hope it helps her to feel less, well, deprived of a friend she's only just met. Give her my love."

"Will do. We must have you and Anjali round for a meal. Once this case is over and I can draw breath maybe."

"That'd be good," John said.

Directly Matt got back to his car he phoned Dilys. "I'm on my way back now. Can you get the team together for a briefing, I think we need to gather all the loose ends together."

"Rightio, sir. Would six o'clock do?"

"That's fine. See you in a minute."

* * *

Just after six o'clock, back at the station, Matt's team were gathered around the main office. They perched on chairs or desks or leant against the wall. They were weary but attentive as Matt outlined what had been done so far, listening to contributions from those who had anything new to report. There wasn't that much, which was frustrating.

"Sara, can you get the info on the Armitages together and match it up with what we got from David Singaram? You've got his report, have you?"

"Yes, sir," Sara said.

"Okay, bring it to me first thing tomorrow. How are you doing, Aidan?"

"I've nearly finished. Do you want me to come and go through it with you?"

"Yes please," Matt said. "Dilys, could you join us?"

Dilys nodded her assent.

"The rest of you, keep going on what's been assigned to you. I know it's a big ask, but if you could all get in as early as possible tomorrow, it would help."

Into Matt's mind came a saying that he always remembered. His first boss when he joined the force, who'd been an experienced and cynical old Londoner, nearing retirement, used to say, 'If you don't make an arrest within the first four days, you can usually whistle for it.' Matt sincerely hoped that wasn't the case – it was now five days since Craig had discovered Geraint's body beneath the balcony. He tried to comfort himself with the fact that it was only two since Dr Curtis's report had revealed it was murder.

Chapter 14

Fabia was coming down the stairs just as Matt came in the front door a few minutes after nine that evening.

"There you are," she said, doing her best not to sound grumpy. She'd been looking forward to him coming home for hours now, although she was perfectly well aware that, in the circumstances, there was little chance of his doing so at a reasonable hour. She spent a lot of her time telling herself off for forgetting what it was like to be in the police force. She, of all people, should understand why Matt kept such long hours, particularly when there was a difficult case on, as this one was.

She put a hand up to Matt's weary face. "You look tired, pet. Have you eaten?"

"I had a sandwich with Dilys and Aidan, but I could do with a glass of wine."

"Coming right up. Red or white."

"Some of that Rioja would be good." He followed her into the kitchen. "I saw John Meredith today, he's Geraint's solicitor. He sends his love."

"How're Anjali and the baby?"

"Fine," he said. "We were saying we must all get together for a meal sometime."

"That'd be nice."

But Fabia was preoccupied. There was something she was very keen to tell him. It had been nagging at her since the day before, but she hadn't had the chance to talk to him about it. She poured Matt his glass of wine, made tea for herself, then they settled in the sitting room and she decided to plunge right in.

"I had a bit of a nosey through some gossip magazines and stuff on the internet."

Matt looked round at her but didn't comment.

"And I think I've found something interesting," Fabia told him.

"To do with what?"

"The case – Geraint," Fabia said, trying not to sound irritated.

"Ah."

There was silence for a moment then Fabia demanded, "Well, do you want to know what it is?"

"Yes, of course," Matt said.

He didn't sound as if he did, but Fabia ignored this and pulled forward her laptop which was on the coffee table in front of them. She tapped away for a moment, then turned it so that Matt could see the screen.

"You see that photo?" she said. "The caption says that it was taken at a fundraising event in Los Angeles, the magazine it came from is called *Entertainment Monthly*, it's dated November 1989. That woman there is Selina Spencer, Geraint's ex-wife."

"Okay, so why do you think this is useful?"

"Well, look at that person there, next to Selina."

Matt leant forward, frowning, then shook his head, "Nah, I don't get it."

"Doesn't it remind you of someone?"

Still frowning, Matt shook his head again and Fabia, impatient, told him what she was thinking. Matt's eyes widened. "I suppose it could be, but how on earth?"

"I don't know, and I may be wrong, but it's worth following up isn't it?"

"It is. You're not often wrong when it comes to faces."

"Thank you," said Fabia smiling. "It's the artist's eye."

"It's not a compliment, just a fact," Matt said.

"That puts me in my place."

"I didn't mean… oh, never mind."

Fabia rested her head on his shoulder. "You're knackered, you poor man."

"Pretty much. Let's call it a day." Matt got up and helped Fabia to her feet.

"I'll be so glad when I can get back to normal," she said ruefully. "It'd be good to be able to stand up without having to be hauled up. Maybe we should invest in a forklift truck."

Matt laughed and put an arm round her as they went towards the stairs. "Not long now," he said, giving her a squeeze.

"I suppose not. I've got an appointment with the practice nurse tomorrow morning. She wants to check up on me and Thumper because of that backache I had."

"Let me know what she says as soon as you've seen her, won't you?"

"I'll text you," Fabia said as she subsided onto their bed.

* * *

Early the following morning Matt sat at his desk feeling frustrated by their lack of progress. When it came to people who would have liked to see the back of Geraint Denbigh, they were, quite frankly, spoilt for choice. Pinning it down to any one person, however, and bringing them here, to Wales, at the right time and place was going to be the devil of a job.

He'd e-mailed both the Hotel de Gersigny and Jacques Hubert in Saint-Malo the day before and was still waiting for replies, but he hadn't checked his e-mails yet. Just as he was running through them, another five or six dropped into the box, and the last one was from Hubert. Matt clicked on it hoping it wasn't just an automatic reply to his e-mail – it wasn't.

> Bonjour, mon ami. It is a long time since I have heard from you. You are well, I hope. To respond to your question about this Stephen Lowe, I have spoken with the manager at the Hotel de Gersigny and he tells me someone of that name stayed at their hotel from Monday to Saturday of last week. I showed to him the photograph you attached to your e-mail and he identified him. I will check with this film producer, Théo Renier, and return to you. Do you wish me to contact the airlines as well? Cordialement, Jacques Hubert.

Well, that seemed to get Lowe off the hook. Matt sat back in his chair and stretched his arms above his head. If this Théo Renier confirmed that Lowe had been working with him, did they really need to check the airlines and ferry services, and the Eurotunnel? Perhaps it would fine, but Jacques had done enough, he would tell him they'd check from this end.

Dilys came into his office just as he was finishing his response to Hubert. "There's an e-mail from David Singaram. Has it come through to you?"

Matt clicked through to his e-mails again and looked at the screen. It was there. "Thanks, Dilys, give me a minute to read through it."

Ten minutes later he went in search of Dilys.

Chapter 15

Because Tenniel had been out of the office for the last two days, and she wanted to speak to him face to face, it wasn't until Thursday morning that Mari had the chance to tackle him. It was just after eight and she'd come into the office early so that she could catch him first thing.

The day before she'd done as much research as she could. Tenniel was rather careless of his privacy online and it didn't take her long to get into his private e-mails. She felt guilty at first, but told herself needs must, and her guilt dissipated when she found some rather revealing e-mails to and from Jason Kennedy, one of which said, 'I'd like you to keep this between us for now, it's best to have it signed and sealed before I discuss it with Mari.' But Jason must have forgotten about that when Mari had taken his call. More fool him. There were also some e-mails between Tenniel and Lydia Phillips, which had made it clear they were in a relationship.

To her relief Tenniel arrived a few minutes later, before anyone else. He breezed into the office, humming as he did so. "*Bore da*," he said, "you're an early bird today." Then he glanced at her, frowned a little, and said, "What's up? You look stressed."

Mari had been dreading confronting him, she hated confrontation, but his attitude stiffened her backbone. For crying out loud, she thought, isn't Geraint's death enough to make me look stressed, let alone anything else?

"I'd like a private word with you," she snapped. "Come into the conference room."

"Can we make it later, I've got–"

"Sorry, Tenniel, it has to be now before anyone else comes in."

This brought him up short. She hardly ever called him Tenniel when they were together, always TD.

"O-kay," he said. "Give me a few minutes and I'll be with you."

"No, now," Mari said.

Picking up some notes she'd made, she strode across the office to the small conference room they used for meetings. Much to her relief, Tenniel followed her and closed the door behind him.

He threw himself into a chair, and draped one arm over the back, the picture of relaxation, but from the tension round his mouth Mari could tell he wasn't nearly as relaxed as he was making out. She sat down opposite him, crossed her arms on the table in front of her and took a deep breath.

"I took a call from Jason Kennedy on Tuesday," she began. Tenniel raised his eyebrows but didn't comment. "From what he said I gather the two of you are co-operating on a new project. He sounded very excited about it. Said it was an option on a book by Lydia Phillips. Is that right?"

Tenniel frowned across at her, chewing at his bottom lip.

"Is that right, Tenniel?" Mari repeated.

He sat forward, smiling at her. "Well, yes. I was going to talk to you about it this week, in fact."

"Were you? And what is this project? And why did you tell Jason you weren't going to tell me about it yet?"

"How did you know I said that?" he asked, no longer smiling.

"Because Jason phoned on Tuesday and blurted it all out. And it seems you're having an affair with Lydia Phillips as well. Now, my understanding was that Geraint had the option on her book, after all, he's known..."

Mari found it hard to go on and cleared her throat. Tenniel started to speak, but she held up a hand to stop him.

"Geraint knew her family from way back. He'd been wanting to make a show about the Rhondda mining communities for ages, and that book was an absolute gift. But he knew how easily influenced she was, and he didn't have much time for her agent. He was going to look after it himself. He talked to me about it, and now I find you stole the project from right under his nose. I gather you persuaded, probably pressured, her to hand the whole thing over to you without even mentioning it to me or my uncle. How could you? How dare you?"

Mari sat glaring across at Tenniel, breathing hard as if she'd been running. Silence reigned for a while then he stretched out a hand to her, but she sat back quickly, not allowing him to touch her. He sighed.

"Look, Mari, I thought it was for the best, and Lydia asked me to take it on. She told me about Geraint's interest but wondered if he was fit enough to continue with it, and I thought not, so that's why she handed it over to me. As it happens, he wasn't fit enough, was he?"

Mari jumped up, rocking her chair back so that it nearly over-balanced, and slapped her hands flat on the table. "He was murdered, you bastard, murdered!" she shouted at him.

"Christ!" Tenniel exclaimed. "Oh God, Mari, I didn't know that."

"Have you been going around this last couple of days with your eyes closed? With your hands over your ears? Well, now you do know." Her voice was shaking. She swallowed back tears and took a deep breath. When she spoke, her voice was quieter but no less contemptuous. "And did you steal *It Could Happen to You* from him as well? Isn't it convenient that someone has got rid of him? Now you can relax and get on with making money out of ideas that Geraint would have run with, would have made a damn sight better job of than you and I will."

"Mari! You're not suggesting—"

"I don't know, I don't know. I just can't believe you've let me down, betrayed me, and shafted my uncle at the same time. Oh, bugger off, TD, just go."

He stood up, looking across at her as he did so, opened his mouth to speak, but she swiped her hand through the air as if trying to swat a fly.

"Go!" she said.

As the door closed behind him, she collapsed into her chair and put her head down on her folded arms. A moment later she searched for her phone, found it under some papers on her desk, and keyed in Cassie's number. She desperately needed to tell her what was happening.

* * *

In her dining room, which doubled as a study, Fabia was trying to work. She stood in front of her easel, chewing at the end of a pencil, as her mind wandered. Having clipped a piece of cartridge paper to the easel, she'd opened her box of Conté pastels and all the other paraphernalia that she'd need for the series of illustrations she'd been commissioned to draw. Everything was neatly arranged on the table beside her. Her agent, Sheena Morley, had e-mailed her to ask how far she'd got, and Fabia had replied that she was well on her way. But that wasn't strictly true, it was just a nice cover-all phrase to keep Sheena happy. However, she desperately wanted to finish this work before the baby arrived, particularly after the news the nurse had given her. She must text Matt and tell him. Still she stood there, gazing at the blank paper without seeing it. All she could think of was what she'd pointed out to Matt the day before and the fact that she wanted to become more involved in the investigation, after all Geraint had been her friend. Okay, that friendship had been short, but she'd still come to care for him. And Auntie Meg would want her to help find his killer, wouldn't she? But the timing, what with the baby and all, wasn't exactly helping.

She thought back to Helen Tudor's visit. Had she said she would be in Cardiff for long? Fabia couldn't remember. But she had left them her mobile number, so would there be any harm in phoning her? Maybe they could meet up and Fabia could ask her… ask her what? Well, about Al Paver for a start. And Selina Spencer's suicide, and Helen's relationship with Geraint. She felt certain Helen was not responsible for his death – her instinct told her that.

Fabia smiled to herself. She and Matt had always differed on the value of instinct as against facts. Matt's inclination was to think along straight lines, rely on what he knew to be true rather than what he simply believed to be so. But Fabia had always relied on instinct and gut reaction. When she worked in the police she'd often been teased about her hunches, but more often than not she'd been proved right. She did, however, feel sure Helen could have told them more than she had. Maybe there were things Helen knew that she wouldn't even realise were relevant.

Before she could chicken out she keyed in Helen's number. There was no response, just a voicemail. She pressed the message icon and tapped in, 'Hi Helen, are you still in Cardiff? Perhaps we could meet up, how about a walk around Gwiddon Park? Or I could come into Cardiff. Let me know, Fabia.' Helen had said she knew the area so she should know the park and the pond. Now Fabia would just have to wait for an answer.

To her relief, it wasn't long in coming. She was in such a hurry to get her mobile out of her pocket that she nearly dropped it. "Hallo?" she said, sounding a little breathless.

"Fabia, it's Helen. Are you okay?"

"I'm fine."

"I got your message. A walk round the park would be lovely." There was a short pause then she said in a rush, "To be honest, there are things I'd like to talk to you about."

"Anything specific?" Fabia asked, trying not to sound too eager.

"I'll tell you when I see you. When did you have in mind?"

"Would this afternoon suit you?"

"Yes, it would," Helen said, and she sounded pleased. "My cousin, Olwen, is out until later and I'm sitting here twiddling my thumbs. Would three o'clock suit you?"

"That'd be fine, and we can come back here for a cup of tea afterwards."

"That sounds lovely. I'll see you later."

Once this was arranged Fabia forced herself back to work. There was absolutely no point in speculating about what Helen had meant, she told herself, although that didn't stop her wondering. But, in the end, she managed to get quite a lot done before glancing at her watch and seeing that it was half past one. She went to the kitchen to heat up some soup for her lunch, then worked on for a while after she'd eaten it.

Just before three Helen arrived. She was huddled up in a pale blue puffa jacket, her fair hair covered in a close-fitting woolly hat. She looked tired and strained. "It's so kind of you to invite me," she said as she stepped into the hall. "I'm not good at sitting doing nothing."

"I know what you mean," Fabia said. "Shall we go straight out?"

"Let's do that, it's brightening up, thank goodness. I'd forgotten how much rain you get around here, but then it wouldn't be so lush and green if you didn't."

The sun had come out and it felt quite warm now. They made their way down Morwydden Lane and across Parc Road, then took to the path that meandered alongside the river Gwyn and around Gwiddon Pond, a bulbous widening of the river as if some giant had taken a scoop out of the land. Fabia loved the colours of the park, the soft velvety brown of the water, the rich brown of the earth on the banks and the jumble of paler colours of the pebbles scattered along the edge. The trees bent down, dipping some branches into the water as it passed as if they were tasting it.

At first they walked without talking, but the silence wasn't relaxed, as if both had things to say but couldn't work out how to begin. Fabia waited for Helen to speak. She didn't want to seem nosey, however much she was in reality, and had decided she shouldn't probe – well, not immediately. But then it occurred to her that Helen might be feeling the same.

Taking a deep breath, Fabia asked, "You mentioned you had something you wanted to talk about."

Helen hunched her shoulders and thrust her hands into the pockets of her jacket. "Yes, I do, but it's difficult to put my finger on what's worrying me. I mean, losing a dear friend is bad enough, but the fact that he's been murdered, that makes it so much worse."

"I know how you feel," Fabia assured her, "and you knew him for so much longer than I did."

"There must be something in Geraint's life that caused someone to kill him. He was such a gentleman. I just can't get my head round it. But it can't have come out of the blue, can it? Unless it was some random lunatic who just stumbled on him."

"No, it can't. I've never had much time for the lone lunatic theory, although I suppose it does happen very occasionally. But in my experience, there's almost always a motive, and a strong one. A friend of mine who was a writer said there was a mantra to every story: who, what, where, when and why. I've always thought that with a crime there's a how, when, why and who. We know more or less how and when, it's the why and who that we have to search for."

"Do you know if your Matt is any further forward?"

"He may be, but he hasn't told me. Sometimes he can't."

"I suppose. It must be awkward at times given that you used to be in the police force."

Fabia gave her a rueful smile. "You could say that. What's more, I used to be his boss."

Helen looked at her, eyebrows raised. "Oh Lord, that must make it that bit more complicated."

"We manage," Fabia said, with a quick grin.

They arrived at the edge of Gwiddon Pond and Fabia suggested they sit on a bench facing the water. She didn't want to admit to it, but her back was aching a bit.

"When did you first meet Geraint?" Fabia asked, thinking this would be a safe way to start.

"We go way back to the early eighties." Helen smiled as if it was a good memory. "We were both living in New York at the time and I got a part in a play he was directing off Broadway. It was so good to meet someone from home. We used to sit and talk about Wales for hours on end. And he needed a friend at the time, it was only a few months after his wife, Beverley, had died in a road accident and he was very low. After that we saw quite a lot of each other until he married Selina, and what a mistake that was."

"In what way?" Fabia asked.

"She hated it if he saw anyone from before they'd met, any of his old friends, including me. He had to concentrate all his attention on her. If he didn't, she'd create the most awful scenes, so gradually we saw less and less of each other. But when they divorced, he got in contact again. He desperately needed someone to hold his hand, to listen, even more so when she committed suicide, which," she said fiercely, "was nothing to do with Geraint, it was not his fault." She banged her hand down on the slats of the bench to emphasise her words. "She'd always been on the edge, very volatile, up one minute, down the next. I think her suicide was much more to do with her existing mental health problems – and her ex, Al Paver – than it was to do with Geraint."

Fabia had listened intently to all that Helen had told her, but at this point she really wanted to ask a question. She took a deep breath and asked, "Why do you say that about Al Paver?"

Helen turned to look at her and Fabia got the impression she was coming back from somewhere in the dark past. "Al?" she asked. "Ah yes, Al." Her tone said much about her opinion of the man. "He was an absolute shit, and that daughter of theirs, I never could like the poor child, although Geraint seemed to be fond of her. He always wanted children."

"But what about Al?"

"He tried to ruin Geraint because of Selina. She'd left him a while before she and Geraint got together, but that didn't mean anything to him. The reason she left Al was that he was controlling, abusive, but he would never accept that she'd moved on, and he kept up this constant drip, drip of poison about Geraint until I don't think she knew what to believe, what was truth and what was lies. Talk about gaslighting! And he turned their own daughter, Rose, against her mother for a while, used her to get Selina back by threatening to stop her seeing the child. But after the divorce Rose went back to live with her mother and I gather they became very close, so when she committed suicide it hit the poor child hard." Helen sighed. "Al was jealous of the close relationship Geraint had with his stepdaughter, so he tried to persuade Selina that it was unnatural, that Geraint was abusing the girl in some way. It was all very messy."

"How awful!" Fabia said.

"Geraint had to threaten to sue Paver before the awful little man shut up. I think Geraint had found out about some of Paver's dodgy business activities and threatened him with making them public."

They sat on for a while watching the ducks and moorhens paddling busily across the pond. Fabia thought back to something she and Matt had talked about the evening before and wondered whether to ask Helen about it. There'd be no harm in doing so, surely. She turned to Helen. "Shall we go back and have that cup of tea?"

"That would be lovely."

"And there's something I'd like to show you."

"Oh? What's that?" Helen asked.

"Better I show you without telling you about it first," Fabia told her, "I don't want you to prejudge it." And they walked slowly back to the house in companionable silence.

Chapter 16

Chief Superintendent Erica Talbot had told Matt she would be down to catch up on his progress at half past four. He'd offered to bring all his information up to her office, but she'd told him it would be more practical if she came down to him. When he'd told Dilys this, she'd smiled and said it was yet another example of the new regime.

In preparation Matt had set up a whiteboard in his office. It would be easier than sitting hunched over in front of a screen, breathing down each other's necks. He'd pinned the names of each of those he thought could be in the frame for Geraint's murder and, after talking it through with Dilys, had listed them from most likely to least. The two of them had marked in the connections between each of the people mentioned on the board, and they'd also included a short explanation of who each person was. He stood in front of it, scowling, his shoulders hunched, his hands deep in his trouser pockets. There was something he knew was missing, but he still couldn't quite accept Fabia's idea. He may mention it, he may not.

He checked his e-mails just in case anything had come in that would cause him to change what he'd outlined, and discovered an e-mail from Jacques Hubert in Saint-Malo confirming that Stephen Lowe had met up with the film producer, Théo Renier, as he'd said and, what was more, they'd found his airline bookings for the relevant dates. It looked as if Lowe could be eliminated from the list. There was also more information from David Singaram in the City of London Police giving a few more details of Jonathan Armitage's financial dealings, but Matt couldn't quite match up these activities with murder, it just seemed over the top. He'd also had checks done with the hotel in Geneva and they'd confirmed that Armitage had been staying there until early on Sunday, but Matt still wasn't sure he could rule him out, given that he could have flown back to Cardiff and returned to Geneva without much trouble and unnoticed by the hotel staff. He put a line through Lowe's name and a question mark beside that of Armitage.

The chief superintendent arrived at exactly half past four. Reluctantly Matt put his phone on silent. He hadn't wanted to do that lately just in case Fabia needed him. He promised himself he'd check for a text or voicemail immediately the meeting was over.

Dilys had come into the room in the wake of the chief and closed the door behind her. The next half hour was spent with Matt going through the motives that each of the people on the whiteboard might have and answering a few pertinent questions from Erica Talbot. She agreed with his assessments of Lowe and Armitage as suspects, and expressed the opinion that Glenda Armitage was unlikely.

"I met her a couple of days ago when I was giving a talk to a local women's aid fundraiser, first talk I've done since I got here." She happened to glance at Dilys and noticed the expression on her face. "That seems to surprise you?"

"Well it does a bit," Dilys admitted, then reddened a little. "Sorry, ma'am, not you being there but Glenda

Armitage. She didn't strike me as someone who'd be involved in that kind of charity work."

"Nor me," said Matt.

"I think she might have been there because she'd made quite a substantial donation to their funds. I got the impression, although I may be wrong, that she enjoyed being the lady bountiful. But when it comes to her brother's death" – she shook her head – "no, quite apart from anything else, I don't think she'd have the strength to lift his body over that balcony rail."

"I think you're probably right," Matt said, "so that leaves us with Brandon Gaunt and Al Paver, or someone we haven't thought of yet. We've managed to track down Gaunt and we're about to set up an interview with him. Paver has proved a little more elusive. Lowe told us he's staying at the Strand Palace in London, and they confirm that. We left a message, but he hasn't come back to us yet. We'll have to set up an interview somehow without frightening him off."

They spent some time going over all the information that the team had turned up while trawling Geraint's manuscript, his diary and paperwork, spreading wide their internet searches, and adding all the information Aidan had retrieved from the various devices, but Matt felt that useful information was thin on the ground. He remembered what Fabia had suggested the evening before and wondered whether he should mention it to the chief. Would she mind that Fabia had done her own research? Given that she'd suggested Fabia might have useful information, and that she'd come up with the idea of Fabia taking on a job with MASH, he thought maybe she wouldn't object as her predecessor would have done. It was hard to get out of the mindset that Charlie Rees-Jones had always imposed of keeping all civilians out of police work, particularly Fabia Havard. For some time he'd sat silent while Erica Talbot and Dilys had talked, but now his boss turned to him.

"You're very quiet, Matt. What's on your mind?" she asked.

Matt pushed a hand through his hair, then sat forward, pushing his doubts aside. "Fabia has been doing some research into Denbigh's background herself."

"Good," she said, to Matt's great relief. "What has she come up with? After all, she knew him."

"Well, it seems that she turned up some information in one of the American entertainment magazines that she thought could be interesting. I'm not sure that it's of any use, but still—"

"She's not often wrong, though, is she?" Dilys said, a little defensively.

With a quick smile at Dilys, Matt said, "True," but he didn't go on.

"Come on then, Matt, spit it out," the chief said, and Matt got the distinct impression she was amused by his hesitancy.

When he told her what Fabia had suggested, she didn't respond immediately, and he waited, wondering what she would say. Dilys too was watching her, waiting for a response. At last it came.

"That sounds very interesting. A bit far-fetched, but still interesting. It'd explain several things that don't exactly fit, wouldn't it? Perhaps you could ask Fabia to show me this photo she found?"

"I'll bring it in first thing tomorrow."

"Okay. Now I must get going." She stood up and so did Matt and Dilys, but as she got to the door, she turned, a slightly mischievous look on her face. "You see, Matt, Fabia would fit right back in here. I must talk to her again about that job idea I had."

* * *

Mari sat in her office trying to concentrate on work. She and Tenniel had barely spoken to each other since their confrontation first thing and she was beginning to feel like getting away from the office whatever the time. In her present state of mind, she really wasn't going to achieve much that was of any use. And what's more, she was worried about Cassie all alone in that big house with no idea of what was going to happen to her. After all, her job as Geraint's carer – she caught herself up, sent a mental apology to Geraint and substituted 'housekeeper' – her job didn't really exist anymore. They'd have to talk about that at some point. But now all Mari wanted to do was to be with Cassie for the comfort and love that she so craved.

Over the past few hours Mari had gone over and over the people that may have had cause to harm Geraint. In spite of Tenniel's behaviour, she couldn't really see him as a murderer. And was what he had done a strong enough motive anyway? Halfway through the afternoon she'd gone back over the diary for the last ten days and had been reminded that on the day Geraint had been killed, she and Tenniel had been in the office all day working together. Surely that ruled him out. Should she mention that to the police? She turned her mind to others who might be suspects. Helen, she discarded immediately. She'd loved Geraint, in fact Mari thought of Helen as his best friend. But there were probably many others who would have been happy enough to see him dead; her mind flinched at the word, but she made herself continue mulling over those who she knew were his enemies. He'd made many of those, but, as far as she was concerned, for the best of reasons – his standards of behaviour had been high, and he gave no quarter when it came to people whose standards didn't match his own.

Rubbing at her tired eyes, she checked the time. It was five o'clock. She turned off her computer, gathered up her bag, her phone and her laptop, and left the office without even telling Tenniel or anyone else that she was going. She just needed to get to Carreg Llwyd House as quickly as possible.

It was nearly an hour after she'd left the office that she arrived at the house. She was glad to see there weren't nearly as many of the paparazzi and media crews around as there had been. She managed to drive past them without drawing too much attention. Some of them took photos as she passed, but there was nothing she could do about that. When she was a few yards up the drive, a uniformed police officer held his hand up to stop her.

"Good afternoon, madam," he said. "Could I have your name, please? We've been told to check arrivals."

"I'm Mari Reynolds, this is— was my uncle's house. I've come to see Cassie Angel."

"Have you any identification? I'm sure you can understand that we're being very careful at the moment." He gave a sideways nod to the crowd at the gate who were now being held back by two of his colleagues.

Mari sighed, rummaged in her bag and got out her driving licence. She handed it to the officer.

He looked at it, nodded again, and said, "Thank you, Ms Reynolds, we'll try to make sure you're not disturbed."

She gave him a tight little smile. "Thanks," she said, and continued up the drive.

Mari parked the car and walked round the house to the kitchen door. She found it locked but her uncle had given her a key a while ago, so she was able to let herself in. There was no sign of Cassie. Mari looked around downstairs but couldn't find her, so she made her way up to the top floor where Cassie had her rooms. She finally found her in her small sitting room, sitting cross-legged on the sofa with her laptop open on her knees.

"Hallo, my love," Mari said, and Cassie jumped up and nearly dropped her laptop.

"Jesus!" she exclaimed, clapping her hand to her chest. "You scared the shit out of me. I thought it was one of those low-lifes from outside."

"I'm sorry," Mari said, going quickly over to Cassie to put her arms round her, but the laptop was in the way.

Cassie pushed it across the sofa and reached out her arms. "Come here, let me give you a proper cuddle."

They settled on the sofa, side by side, Cassie's arm round Mari protectively.

"Those bastards are still out there," Mari said.

"I know, but the police are keeping them under control. I forgot to tell you earlier on, one of the paps crept round to the kitchen door yesterday and I whacked him. I think I broke his nose, I certainly trashed his camera. He won't do that again."

"Cassie!" Mari gasped. "Did you hurt yourself?"

"No, but I certainly hurt him," Cassie said with satisfaction.

"You're amazing," Mari said. "Will there be repercussions?"

"Nah, he was trespassing. All in a day's work," Cassie replied and grinned at her.

They sat in companionable silence for a while, then Mari turned to look at Cassie. "After I spoke to you, I spent some time checking up on what Tenniel's been doing, well, what he was doing on the day Geraint was killed, and I don't think he could have killed Geraint. We were in meetings all day, and we started really early, about seven thirty."

"I suppose he could have come to the house really early, before work."

"But I just don't think it's likely. Wouldn't all the... everything happening have woken you?"

"I was in Cardiff that day," Cassie said, "and I got going very early."

"But I know him too well, I just don't think he'd have the courage. And I'm absolutely certain Helen had nothing to do with it, which leaves one of those shitty men. Two of them visited Geraint recently, didn't they?"

"Yes," Cassie said. "Stephen Lowe and Brandon Gaunt. I made sure that he told me their names so that I could block them if they phoned on the landline."

"The thing is – whoever it was – how did they persuade him to go up to the balcony? Oh, Cassie, it's all so dreadful, I can't bear it."

She turned to bury her face in Cassie's shoulder and began to cry. Cassie just stroked Mari's hair and waited for her to recover herself.

Slowly the sobs quietened and then Mari lifted her head and rummaged in her pocket for a tissue. "Sorry, it's just been so awful."

"I know, I know." Cassie soothed her, rubbing her hand up and down Mari's back. "It's been a really shitty few days and it'll probably get worse before it gets better. But it will be over one day, you know that, and although you'll always miss him, I will too, it'll become easier to bear, believe me."

"I think it'll be easier when we know what bastard is responsible," Mari said, sounding very unlike her usual quiet self. "One person I think might have something to do with it is that bloody Al Paver man. He actually accused Geraint of abusing Selina's little girl. Can you imagine? And then, when Selina committed suicide, he blamed Geraint again, the shit."

"Isn't Paver in the US?" Cassie said. "I don't see how–"

"But he could have come to the UK, couldn't he? I'm going to mention him to the chief inspector, suggest he finds out where he is."

"Wouldn't he have thought of that? They took Geraint's manuscript away. He was probably mentioned in it."

Mari didn't respond immediately, just sat chewing at her bottom lip and frowning at nothing in particular, then she said, "But the more I think about it, the more I'm convinced he had something to do with Geraint's death. He tried to ruin him, Cassie. Geraint was telling me about him a while ago, and Helen's told me a bit as well. I really think I should mention it to Chief Inspector Lambert, don't you?"

"It doesn't seem very likely, but let's not think about it now," Cassie said briskly as she pushed herself up from the sofa. "I'm going to get us a good stiff gin and tonic each, and then I'm going to fix us something to eat. And you're going to eat whether you like it or not, so none of that 'I couldn't touch a thing' nonsense, my girl."

Ten minutes later Cassie was back with a brimming glass chinking with ice, a slice of lime floating in it. "There you are," she said, "get that down you. And what would you like to eat?"

"I would actually love an omelette."

"Omelette coming up then."

"Oh Cassie, what would I do without you?"

Cassie smiled down at her. "I've no idea," she said as she left the room.

* * *

Now Mari had thought about Al Paver she couldn't get him out of her mind. The police might have missed mention of him in Geraint's autobiography. There'd be no harm in suggesting they check on him, would there? Helen had suggested she speak to them, although that had been about Tenniel's activities. She decided to think about it. She'd go and give Cassie a hand with their meal.

Mari pushed herself up from the sofa and, in doing so, knocked Cassie's laptop on to the floor. She bent to pick it up and as she lifted it, it opened and the screen came alive. It showed a half-finished e-mail. All she noticed at first was the address at the top, maybe because the name had been so much in her mind: al.paver53@gmail.com. Then her eyes travelled down to the greeting at the top of the e-mail. 'Darling Dad' it said. Darling *Dad*?

A feeling like ice cold water ran through her body. What on earth? Shaking and cold, she read through the first paragraph. There was no escaping the meaning of it

145

all. There was no room for doubt. None. She pushed the laptop on to the coffee table and slammed it shut. But that made no difference. She couldn't unsee what she'd seen. And she'd said that she wanted to speak to the police. But what she had to tell them now was very different to what she'd intended. How could she tell them…? No, it wasn't possible. She paced up and down, hugging her arms round her body as the minutes ticked by. Almost without realising it, she searched in her handbag for the card that woman police officer had given her. What was her name? Sergeant Dilys something. Taking her mobile out of her pocket, with trembling fingers she keyed in the number on the card.

The call was picked up on the second ring and Mari stumbled into speech. "It's Mari Reynolds– I– I'm at my uncle's house, please can you come? Come yourself– now– I think I've found out something, about… about his death– murder, you see I–"

But at that moment Cassie came back into the room.

Chapter 17

It wasn't until Matt arrived home, early for once, that Fabia remembered she'd not texted him with her news. While she was preparing a chicken for roasting, stuffing it full of chopped-up lemon and sprigs of thyme, she said casually, as if it didn't matter a jot, "By the way, the nurse, and the doctor for that matter, because the nurse called her in, both think we've got my due date wrong. Because of the baby's size and position they think it's more like thirty-eight weeks than thirty-six. A bit of a relief, really. Not so long to wait."

"You should have texted me, Fabia," Matt said, frowning. "You're always going on at me about keeping in contact, now you're at it."

"I know. I'm sorry. It's just been a busy day what with Helen here and all, and she agrees with me, by the way, about that photo."

"I mentioned it to the chief. She said she thought it was a bit far-fetched." He glanced at Fabia's face and added quickly, "But she also said she'd like to see the photo. She asked me to bring it in."

"Good. I've got a strong feeling about this."

He put his arms round her. "You and your feelings."

"Well, I'm often right, aren't I?" she said, looking up at him with a grin.

"True. I have to admit you are."

Fabia turned back to the chicken, deciding it was time to change the subject. "This is nearly ready to go in the oven. What's up? You don't look happy."

"I've got to go to London tomorrow, that's why I got home a bit earlier than usual," Matt said. "It's a bloody nuisance."

"Why have you got to go?"

Matt sat down at the kitchen table and leant on it with folded arms. "That Al Paver bloke, Selina Spencer's ex, is staying at the Strand Palace Hotel. He's the one Stephen Lowe suggested would be worth interviewing, you know, when he came to brag about all his alibis. I've fixed it with the Met and I've managed to fix an interview with Brandon Gaunt in the afternoon. I'm going up first thing, taking Sara Gupta with me."

"Why not Dilys?"

"I want her here in charge while I'm out of the office, and I thought it would be good experience for Sara. She's a Londoner so she'll know her way around."

"Has anything else turned up today?" Fabia asked as she put the chicken in the oven.

"Anything else? Well, Aidan has found out that most of the shitty e-mails and phone calls came from local sources, although he hasn't pinpointed exactly where. That complicates things a bit, unless Geraint's sister decided to wind him up, but I really can't see her doing that."

"You never know."

"True. Alternatively, it could have been his brother-in-law, worried that Geraint might step on his financial toes. I don't know. I'm just hoping Aidan will be able to narrow it down a bit more."

"Did you get anything useful from the security cameras?" Fabia asked as she sat down opposite him.

"Unfortunately, no. There's a snatch of film when Stephen Lowe followed Craig round the house to the garden which pinpoints when he visited Geraint, but it just confirms that he was telling the truth, about that anyway. There are serious gaps, the system wasn't exactly state of the art."

"Was it tampered with, perhaps?"

"Could be, but it's difficult to work out who could have done so."

Fabia glanced at him then away. "Well, if I was right…"

Matt gave her a sideways look. "It's a big if, but I have set one of the team to do some deeper research, and of course, we have the interviews with Paver and Gaunt tomorrow which could give us more information. Maybe one of them will confess, we'll make an arrest, and that will be that."

Fabia laughed. "Since when have you been living in fantasy land?"

Matt grimaced and said, "I have this gut feeling – don't laugh – that it has something to do with him, and given what Geraint said about him and his relationship with Selina, and his attempt to destroy Geraint, it wouldn't surprise me at all if we found that he was responsible. Dilys says he's the one who Geraint was most trenchant about in his autobiography." Matt got up and took Fabia's hand. "Come on, let's go and watch some mindless TV until the chicken's ready. Dilys says there's a new police drama on Netflix, I want to watch it and see how many things they get wrong."

But Matt didn't have a chance to turn the television on as a call came through from Dilys. Fabia sat listening to his side of the conversation.

"How long ago was this? … And you think the phone was left on deliberately? … Yes. Do we still have a presence up there? … That's hardly adequate. We'd better get out there as fast as possible … Okay. David Hywel should still be up there, get through to him and tell him to wait for us. Do you think there's any chance we can take them by surprise? ... Yes, you're probably right. Pick me up on your way."

As Matt cut off the call Fabia could no longer contain her curiosity. "What on earth is going on, Matt?"

"It looks as if Cassie Angel has gone off on one again. Remember she attacked that reporter? Well it seems she's now gone for Mari Reynolds."

"What? Why on earth? I thought they were–" Then Fabia's eyes opened wide. "Oh, I see. It seems I might be right."

"It does indeed, my darling," Matt said ruefully. "Apparently Dilys got a call from Mari who said she'd found out something about her uncle's murder. She sounded as if she was in a panic and begged Dilys to send someone or come herself. But then Dilys said there was a noise, a sort of thump, as if the phone had been dropped, but she could still hear voices, muffled at first but then louder. It sounded like quite some confrontation. Someone screamed, 'He's my Dad, you stupid bitch.'"

"Cassie?"

"Looks like it. After that there were sounds of some kind of fight and someone screamed. Then a moment later the phone was switched off."

"But haven't you got someone out there keeping an eye?"

"Yes, a few, but only on the gate, to keep the press pack in check. Most of them have decided to leave, so we thought it would be okay to take the others off the job earlier on today. We desperately needed personnel for a serious incident in Newport."

"Oh Matt, even with Erica Talbot's promise to let you have more staff?" Fabia asked.

"There's a limit, Fabia, as you well know."

"I know, I know, I'm not criticising you, nor am I going to say I told you so. It's all too awful." Fabia looked stricken, but soon turned to practicalities. "Is your phone well charged?"

Matt took it out of his pocket, glanced at the screen. "Yes, for once."

"I'll make you a sandwich to take with you, I doubt you'll be back any time soon."

"You're a gem, my love," Matt said as he followed her out to the kitchen.

Quickly she made him a ham sandwich, put it into a plastic container, added an apple and a banana, and gave it to Matt.

"I could have done that for myself," he remarked, with a grin.

"You could, but I need to keep busy when stuff like this happens."

Matt put an arm round Fabia's shoulders. "There's no way I can take you on this jaunt so don't even ask."

"I wasn't going to, Matt," Fabia said, a little testily. "Heavily pregnant women are definitely not allowed. I can see that. But please, please, keep me posted."

"I'll do my best." He kissed her gently. "Why don't you get an early night? You certainly need the rest."

"For goodness sake, Matt! It's only just half past five," Fabia protested. "I'll get down to some work once I've eaten, there's plenty I have to get on with and it'll keep me occupied."

It wasn't long before there was a knock at the front door and Matt let Dilys in. She was looking tired but determined.

"Hi Fabia, sorry about this," she said, and to Matt, "I've roped in Sara, Tom and Dave, and two from uniform. From what I heard I think we may need plenty of support."

"Good," said Matt. "Let's get going."

Fabia stood in the doorway and watched them leave. She felt suddenly apprehensive. She had a strong feeling this wasn't going to be an easy call.

* * *

Matt and Dilys arrived at Carreg Llwyd House at about the same time as the rest of the team. They were deeply relieved to see that the press pack was no longer in evidence.

"Quiet everybody, as quiet as possible," Matt said. "Okay, Dave and Sara, I'd like you round the back of the house and keep an eye on the kitchen door, and you, Reuben" – he indicated one of the uniformed officers – "go round the side to the French windows that give on to the lawn. Dilys with me; the rest of you, back us up."

He walked to the front door and rang the bell. There was no response. He knocked on the solid wood of the door and this time he heard the dogs beginning to bark. "Hell," he said, "I'd forgotten about those Dobermanns."

"I've done the dog training course, sir, that might help," David Hywel told him.

"Good, David, stay close," Matt said, and lifted his hand to the doorbell again. This time he shouted, "It's the police, Miss Angel. Would you open the door please?"

Yet again there was no response other than the dogs.

"From what I can hear, I'd say the dogs are at the back of the house, which is all to the good for now," Matt said. "Dilys, can you try Mari's phone? There's always a possibility she might pick up the call."

Dilys did as he asked but all she got was a mechanical voice telling her that the person was unable to take her call. She tried the landline, but it rang and rang then was picked up by the answerphone, and she looked up Cassie's mobile number, but that went to voicemail as well.

"A bit of a stand-off isn't it, sir," she said to Matt.

He didn't comment as, at that moment, Reuben Trent came hurrying round the corner of the house to the front door where they were gathered.

"Sir, sir," he called softly as he approached. "I tried the French windows and they aren't locked. We could get in that way."

"Well done, Reuben. Yes, we could," Matt said. "Dilys, you come with me. The rest of you, be ready if things kick off."

But before Matt and Dilys could make their way round to the side of the house, they heard a sash window pushed up with a crash just above their heads. Matt stepped back in order to see who was there and what he saw made him freeze to the spot. Cassie Angel was leaning with her elbows on the sill, both hands wrapped round a wicked-looking revolver.

"You can fucking well leave, and right now, or I'll use this," Cassie said, her normally calm voice tinged with hysteria.

Both Matt and Dilys froze in their tracks then slowly held up their hands. Around them the others did the same. Matt said as calmly as he could, "We were just looking for Mari Reynolds. Is she with you?"

"Yes, and she's not leaving, but you lot are." She waved the gun around to indicate that she meant all of them.

"Okay, okay," Matt said, keeping his voice low and level; his hands still in the air. "We'll leave now if that's what you want, but could we speak to Mari first?"

"Go away! Go away! Fucking go away!" she screamed at them, and slowly they all backed away.

The only two who were left were Sara Gupta and Dave Parry by the kitchen door and, once they'd moved back far enough to be out of sight of the window Cassie was leaning from, Dilys radioed them and told them what was happening. Luckily all the vehicles were also out of that window's line of sight, but there was no knowing if she'd choose another one so, within a few minutes, obeying Matt's low-voiced and rapid instructions, they all piled into the cars and made their way back down the drive until they were completely hidden from view, parked up on the grass verge by the gate.

Immediately they were stationary, Matt got on to headquarters, while the others stood around exclaiming about the developments and discussing tactics.

"You've got your taser, haven't you?" Dave asked.

"Yup, definitely."

"Was this expected?"

"No. The boss wouldn't have brought us all here if it had been." This from Sara who indulged in a bit of hero worship when it came to Matt.

Quickly Matt explained the situation and asked for help from the joint firearms unit. "How long do you think it'll take? Do you know where they are right now?" he asked. "Cwmbran. Right ... Twenty minutes give or take? Good, good." Then, at Dilys's prompting, he asked for a crisis negotiator. "We'll stand by here. I hope our apparent absence will have calmed her down for now. We really need to know if Mari Reynolds is alright. Get the chief super to contact me here."

After this they began to set up the blue and white barrier tape, but other than that all they could do was wait. Tom Watkins and Dave Parry had offered to try to get around to the back of the house, but Matt vetoed this. Although it would have been possible, he wasn't having them going off on their own.

"I don't want any of you taking unnecessary risks. We'll have no heroics under my watch," he said firmly.

Both Tom and Dave looked a little disappointed.

Matt turned to Dilys. "Tell me again about that call from Mari."

"From the little I heard," she told Matt, "I'm sure as I can be that Mari was very scared. I could hear her voice trembling with the few words she managed to say. Then there was a sound like someone had been slapped, and I heard her cry out, at least I'm pretty sure it was her, then the noise like I told you, of the phone being dropped. Not long after that the call was cut off."

Matt's mobile rang. He listened intently for a few minutes, then said, "She's coming from where? Pontypool? Then she should arrive not long after the AFOs … Okay, thanks."

Dilys was waiting patiently, but her eyebrows were raised in query as she looked at Matt.

"The crisis negotiator, her name's Paige Roberts," he said, "do you know her?"

Dilys frowned in concentration. "I think I do. Yes," she said as her face cleared. "I came across her last year, that kid who was threatening to jump from the footbridge, she talked him down. She's a tidy sort, good at her job."

A while later, in the distance, they could hear the faint noise of sirens. This faded out and then, minutes later, two police BMWs drew up and parked, and two authorised firearms officers jumped out of each one.

Chapter 18

Fabia could settle to nothing. However hard she tried to work at her easel, time and again she found herself standing, gazing at nothing and wondering what Matt was up to. In the end she decided to give up. She'd done too much of this pacing up and down waiting for Matt to phone lately. I really ought to be able to switch off, she thought, it's such a ridiculous waste of time and energy.

She glanced at her watch. Just after half past six. She decided to phone Cath Temple. Picking up the handset, she punched in the number and waited, leaving her mobile free in case Matt phoned or texted her. Within a couple of rings, the call was picked up.

"Hallo, pet, I was just thinking about you," Cath said. "I've just finished a confirmation class and I was going to phone you once I'd got myself a glass of wine."

"Please don't mention wine. I've been so good keeping off the booze while I've been pregnant but there is a limit."

"Poor you, but not long now."

"No, just two weeks."

"Two weeks? I thought you had another four to go."

"The doctor thinks it's nearer than that, and I've been having a lot of backache. What do contractions feel like?"

"I don't really know," Cath said. "Since I used to be a nurse in a past life, I've been present at a lot of births, but you really can't tell unless it happens to you, and that's not going to happen with me, is it?"

Fabia could hear regret in her voice. "Oh, I don't know, you're only forty after all, and look at me."

"But you've got to find the man first, haven't you?"

"True." Fabia thought it time to change the subject. "Matt's out on a job and I just can't concentrate on work. I'm so restless."

"Do you want some company? Shall I come round to yours?"

"That'd be great. I've got a chicken roasting in the oven if you're interested," Fabia said. "I'd love to have some company."

"Your roast chickens are legendary, I can't wait. And you can tell me when I get there what Matt's up to."

"Will do. See you in ten minutes."

* * *

The AFOs had joined Matt and Dilys and the rest of his team.

"Sergeant Floyd Amory," an older officer introduced himself. He was a stocky, dark-skinned man who looked to be in his early forties. "This is Constable Rhian Seddon." Seddon was red-haired, freckled, and had a don't-mess-with-me look to her. Amory also introduced the other two officers then asked, "What's the situation, sir?"

Before Matt had time to respond, a red Fiat pulled up and a woman in plain clothes joined them. Dilys greeted her and explained who they all were, then introduced her to Matt as Paige Roberts.

Matt gave all the new arrivals a quick outline of what had happened so far. "We think that Mari Reynolds is in there against her will. Although she and Cassie Angel are

157

in a relationship, it looks as if something has happened or been said that's scuppered that. We suspect that Cassie's real name is Rose Spencer and that she is the daughter of Geraint Denbigh's ex-wife."

"Blow me, this is complicated," exclaimed Floyd Amory. "So why do you think she's gone apeshit?"

"I know it sounds far-fetched, but my partner, Fabia Havard, is an artist and…"

Amory gave a low whistle. "Fabia Havard's involved?"

"Yes," Matt said, rather curtly, expecting the usual remarks about Fabia having been suspected of corruption and thrown out of the force, but they didn't come.

Amory grinned and said, "Well, well, I used to work with her way back, she's a tidy sort, is Fabia, she didn't deserve the shit they threw at her. You're a lucky man. But what's this about her being an artist?"

"That's what she's been doing since she retired," Matt told him, feeling relieved that his view of Fabia was a positive one. "She was doing some unofficial research into Geraint Denbigh's past life, he was a friend of hers, and she came across a photo of his ex, Selina Spencer, with her daughter, who was about eleven at the time. She's convinced that Cassie Angel, Denbigh's housekeeper, and that child, Rose Spencer, are one and the same person."

"And if that proves to be the case, you suspect she was responsible for his death?"

"We do, but it's going to be hellish difficult to prove," Matt said.

"How do you want to proceed?" Amory asked Matt.

"We've tried both women on their mobiles and the landline, but there's been no response to any of them. We'll keep trying, if you could be in charge of that, Sara."

"Will do, sir," Sara said.

"We have no way of knowing if Mari Reynolds is hurt or not," Matt told them, "and if she is okay, we don't know how long that will be the case. It's imperative that we get into the house as soon as possible to ensure her safety. We do know that Cassie Angel – I'll keep to that name to avoid confusion – has a handgun but we have no idea what calibre it is, we were too far away to tell. As I told you, she threatened us from a first-floor window, but there's no knowing where they might be in the house now. One thing we do know is that the French windows into the sitting room on the left-hand side of the house were unlocked earlier on, but she could have locked them by now."

"Seems to me a softly-softly approach would be best to start with," Sergeant Amory said.

"I agree," said Matt. "The driveway curves just before you come to the house so we wouldn't be seen until we're virtually at the front door. Obviously, you'll use your cars, your ARVs, since they're fully equipped. You'll come with us, Paige, we're going to need you."

"Can you give me a few more details on who is who?" Paige asked.

"Could you bring Paige up to speed, Dilys?" Matt said.

"Will do, sir."

The two women stepped aside, and Paige made notes while Dilys gave her details of the case so far.

Meanwhile Matt deployed Tom Watkins, David Hywel and the young constable called Reuben to stand guard just inside the gates. After consultation with Floyd Amory, he asked Dave Parry and the other uniformed officer to get around the back of the house through the garden, but only if they could do so without being seen from the house.

At last they were ready. The direct radio link to command at headquarters had been set up and Matt was in radio contact with Chief Superintendent Erica Talbot. The AFOs got into their cars, and Matt, Dilys and Paige into theirs. By this time Matt calculated that they had about another half hour of daylight to work in, but he had a feeling this could be an all-nighter. He realised he hadn't spoken to Fabia since they'd arrived so, since Dilys was going to be driving, he took out his mobile to give her a quick call. She picked up almost before the phone had time to ring.

Without giving her a chance to say anything, he said, "Fabia, this looks as if it's going to be a long haul." He gave her a brief explanation of what was happening. "I probably won't get home until the early hours, if then."

There was a short pause, then Fabia said, "Don't worry, but keep me posted, and don't take any risks."

She sounded rather odd and Matt asked, "Are you okay?"

"Yes, yes, I'm fine," she said, sounding a little too bright and breezy. "Cath's come round and we're having a catch-up. But Matt, be careful, won't you?"

"Absolutely," he said, putting more confidence into the word than he felt. "I've got to go now. Love you." Frowning, he cut off the call.

"Trouble at home, sir?" Dilys asked.

"No, I don't think so," but he wasn't too sure.

* * *

Fabia put her mobile in her pocket as Cath asked, "Why didn't you tell him your waters have broken?"

"I couldn't. They've got a shooter to deal with."

Cath gasped.

"They've had to call in the AFOs," Fabia told her.

"Who are they?"

"Authorised firearms officers." Fabia leant on the back of a chair, breathing deeply. "And a crisis negotiator, the whole shebang," she said a moment later.

"Okay," said Cath decisively. "You've had, what? Only a couple of contractions so far and they're pretty far apart but, given your age–"

Fabia grunted in disgust, but Cath ignored it.

"Given your age," she repeated firmly, "and the fact that this has all kicked off a bit earlier than you anticipated, I'm going to take you into the hospital right now. Have you got your bag packed?"

"Yes, I did it earlier on today. I suddenly got the urge to be ready for anything," Fabia said, giving her friend a lopsided grin. "I got the cradle sorted and everything, and I cleaned the bathroom."

"A sure sign. It's called nesting," Cath told her.

Fabia sat down at the table and put her head down on her folded arms. "This isn't the way I wanted it to be, Cath. I wanted Matt to be with me." The words came out in a muffled wail.

Cath put a hand on her shoulder. "I know, pet, but babies don't know about timetables and all that. They do their own thing. Now, come on, let's get that bag of yours and get going. We'll give Matt a ring when you've been assessed, and we know what's happening."

Fabia sat back, shoulders sagging. "I know you're right," she said as she pushed herself up from the chair. "I'll get my bag."

In a moment Fabia was back downstairs. "I'll just leave Matt a note, in case I can't get hold of him. I don't want to leave him a text, if he reads it it'll distract him."

She pulled a piece of paper towards her from the random pile of odds and ends on the kitchen table, scribbled for a couple of minutes, weighted the note down with an empty mug, then straightened and took a deep breath.

"Okay," she said to Cath, giving her friend a brave grin. "You're an absolute gem, my friend. What would I do without you?"

"Heaven knows," said Cath.

"Shouldn't I phone the hospital or something first?" Fabia asked.

"No. Waste of time trying to get through. Okay, let's get this show on the road."

While they were driving into Newport, Cath tried to persuade Fabia to text Matt and tell him what was happening, but she wouldn't.

"I can't, Cath, I really can't. I know what it's like when you've got a shooter to deal with. He needs to have his whole mind on the job, not be worrying about me. Anyway, I doubt that anything much is going to happen for hours." Another contraction gave the lie to her words, but she tried her best to sound confident and unperturbed when she'd breathed her way through it. "You're with me, what more could I want?"

"And I'm staying until Matt arrives," Cath said decisively.

Fabia said nothing in reply. She was feeling a little tearful, but she told herself to stop being a wimp and grinned at Cath instead.

* * *

Evening was drawing in and, even though it had been a sunny day, the light had faded fast. It was almost dark now. They had driven slowly, in convoy as far as the curve in the driveway. Matt knew that he'd have to leave the four AFOs to make the decision on when to move further up towards the house, they were the experts after all, but he felt frustrated at not being able to call the shots, caught as he was between them and the command centre.

Sara had kept trying the three numbers, Cassie and Mari's mobiles and the landline. She'd just tried Cassie's again, with no result, and then she punched in Mari's number once more. At last, there was a response. A trembling voice said, "It's me, Mari."

Matt saw Sara's eyes widen as she held up a hand to attract his attention. They all listened intently as Sara put her phone on speaker and asked, "Can you talk?"

Both Floyd Amory and Matt signalled for complete quiet around her.

"Please help me, please," Sara heard Mari say in a trembling whisper, but those close enough to her managed to hear it.

"Is Cassie with you?"

"No. She's gone to the kitchen. She said she wanted a drink."

"Has she still got the gun?"

"Yes. She took it with her. She'll be back in a minute."

Amory had been scribbling a note. Now he held it up so that Sara could read it. He'd written, 'suggest that she puts the phone down but leaves it on.'

"We'll get you out of there as soon as we can. Put the phone down and leave it on. Which room are you in?"

"We're downstairs, in the sitting room," Mari whispered, then, "Shit, shit, shit, she's coming back."

"Don't turn your phone off. Leave it on. Just put it down, put it down," Sara said firmly and clearly.

She held her mobile up so that everyone could hear as much as possible. They could just make out a door opening and a voice saying, "There we are, I've brought coffee." It was as if this was a social occasion. "That's what you need."

Matt and Dilys recognised the voice as Cassie's.

Chapter 19

Inside the house Mari sat on one of the armchairs in the sitting room, her feet curled up under her and the mug of coffee, which she hadn't touched, held in one trembling hand. She pressed the mug down on the arm of the chair to avoid slopping the liquid all over herself and looked across the room at Cassie, who was pacing up and down like a panther in a cage, the gun back in her hand.

"What the hell are they doing out there?" Cassie muttered.

Mari stayed quiet. This was not a question she could answer. She glanced quickly across at the table where she had hastily put down her phone when Sara told her to. Cassie didn't seem to have noticed it in the ten minutes since she'd come back into the room.

Suddenly Cassie turned and looked straight at Mari. "You see I had to do it. You do see that, don't you?"

Mari found herself shaking her head, but she said nothing, what could she say?

"Of course, I had to get to know Geraint first, sort of lull him into a false sense of security, then I could tell him how he ruined my mom's life. I remembered him from when I was small, but I hadn't seen him since then. It wasn't until my dad told me all about him that I realised what a dreadful man he was. Dad told me everything, Mari, everything. How Geraint was unfaithful to my poor mother again and again, how he used to hit her. How he played on her weaknesses and then just walked out on her. That was why she killed herself. It was all his fault. He might as well have killed her himself."

Mari shook her head and made a little sound of protest, and Cassie swung round on her, almost snarling.

"It's true, you stupid woman, all true. He – killed – my – mom," she shouted, spitting out the words one by one. "You have to understand, I had to search him out, avenge her in some way."

"But... but you didn't have to kill him," Mari said, her voice catching on a sob.

"Yes I did." She scowled at Mari. "Apart from anything else, I was afraid he'd find out I'd sold some of his precious artwork."

"Cassie!" Mari couldn't stop herself asking, "What did you sell?"

"Never you mind."

"But how could you kill– harm him once you'd got to know him?" Mari could feel the tears gathering in her throat. "He was fond of you, Cassie. He told me so."

"Fond. Fond! He was not. He treated me like a skivvy."

"No!" Mari protested.

"Yes!" Cassie shouted, then she laughed. "But I got my own back. Got lots of dosh from that stuff I sold, and watched him get more and more doddery because of the drugs. I wanted to wait for the best moment. And that's what I did." Cassie stared across at Mari from the other side of the table. "Drink your coffee."

Mari lifted her mug and took a gulp. It stuck in her throat, but she managed to swallow it down.

"But what about us, Cassie?" Mari couldn't stop herself asking.

Cassie didn't look at her. "Yea, well, that was unfortunate. It's not what I intended, but–" She shrugged and began her pacing once again.

Mari shivered and wrapped her arms round her body. Then she glanced at the table and gave a sigh of relief. Cassie hadn't noticed the phone. Not yet.

"It was that so-called autobiography of his," Cassie said. "He kept telling me bits and pieces of what he was writing. He didn't mention Mom much, probably felt too guilty, but he did say some awful things about my father. Al Paver was a deceitful shit, Al Paver was a liar and responsible for my mom's death. How dare he? It made me so angry! I knew then that I wanted to kill him, but I couldn't until I'd stopped him writing that shitty autobiography, telling all those lies about Dad."

Mari burst out, "But were they lies?" and regretted what she'd said immediately the words were out of her mouth.

"How dare you suggest my father's a liar?" Cassie shrieked. "How dare you?"

She lunged at Mari who cowered back, her eyes screwed tight shut, expecting a blow or a shot at any moment, but neither happened. She dared to open her eyes and saw that Cassie was standing over her, breathing in deep gasps. But the gun was no longer in her hand, it was on the table just next to Mari's phone.

Cassie said, "No," as if talking to herself. "No," she said again, then muttered, "Self-control, most important."

Then the pacing began again but the gun stayed where it was.

"He was so arrogant, so full of himself, so I decided I'd give him something to worry about." Cassie gave a sharp little laugh, but there was no humour in it. "All those e-mails and phone calls, and he had no idea they were coming from inside his own house. No idea at all. Brilliant, don't you think?"

She looked at Mari, her eyes wide. "Don't you?" she demanded.

"I... I don't know. I–"

But Cassie was no longer listening. "That stroke of his was a godsend. It gave me the idea. I've always kept up to date with what he was doing, what was happening in his life. I've got piles and piles of stuff about him on my laptop." She sounded very proud of this. "You see, I knew one day I'd find him and then I could... I could deal with him. So, when I saw all the news about him having a stroke and then moving back to Wales, I thought, why don't I follow him? Of course, getting this job was such a stroke of luck, but then I thought, it's meant to be. The fact that I got it, well, it was sort of confirmation that I was doing the right thing. I knew it was up to me to get revenge."

"But why, Cassie, why?" Mari pleaded, unable to stop herself asking the question.

"Aren't you listening? Haven't I told you already? Because he killed my mother. An eye for an eye." She was standing right over by the French windows now, staring across the room at Mari, then she turned to look out of the window.

Almost without thinking and before she could stop herself, Mari sprang forward and grabbed the gun. She jumped up, stood behind the table and, holding the gun in a trembling hand, screamed at Cassie, "Get out! Get out! I'll shoot! I will!"

A moment later all hell broke loose. Cassie launched herself across the room at Mari at the same moment that the French windows crashed open. Breaking glass sprayed across the floor. Mari leapt back but the armchair was in the way. She fell backwards and the gun jerked in her hands. A shot rang out. Mari could hear screaming, didn't know if it was her or Cassie. She curled up in the chair, shut her eyes tight and put her hands over her ears, then realised the gun was still in her hand.

There were shouts of "Armed police!" and "Put the gun down! Put the gun down!" repeated several times. She let go of it and it fell with a clatter to the floor. Then there was more shouting. "Hands above your heads! Hands above your heads now!"

Mari lifted her hands and opened her eyes.

The room seemed to be full of police dressed in black armour. At first, they were crouched behind a big shield, but she could see that they were armed and pointing their weapons into the room.

Cassie was crouched on the rug in front of the fireplace, her hand clutching her shoulder. Blood was oozing between her fingers. "You lousy bitch!" she screamed.

Very slowly one of the police officers moved forward, his gun still at the ready. The others stayed where they were, guns pointing both at Mari and Cassie. Then the officer who had moved further into the room reached down and picked up the gun.

* * *

An hour later Mari was curled up on the sofa in the sitting room, cradling a cup of hot, sweet tea in her hands. Sara Gupta was beside her taking down a full statement. When it had been suggested they could wait until the following day, Mari had insisted she wanted to get it over with now, before she went home.

"Do you live alone?" Sara asked.

"Yes, although I used to spend a lot of time here." As she spoke, tears began to trickle down her cheeks.

"You really shouldn't be on your own after all that's happened. Is there anyone we can call to be with you?"

Mari wiped at her face with the back of her hand and frowned as if she didn't understand the question, then said, "I suppose I could call my mother. She lives in Caerleon. But she might not want to come."

"Give me her number. I'll call her for you. She'll come," Sara said. Coming from a loving family, she was unable to imagine that a mother would not want to support her daughter at a time like this.

Mari hesitated. "I don't think—"

"I'm sure she would want to be with you," Sara said firmly.

As if she hadn't the strength to protest, Mari gave Sara the number and listened as Sara spoke to Glenda, wondering in a detached sort of way what her mother's reaction actually was. But it seemed that Sara had got through to her.

"She says she'll be here in half an hour to pick you up," Sara told her, then stretched her arms out to hold Mari as she finally broke down and cried as if she would never stop.

Dilys came over to check that Sara could cope, but Sara gave her a quick smile as she continued to hold Mari's shaking body and mouthed, "Leave her to me."

Dilys nodded and left Sara to it, telling herself she'd mention Sara's behaviour to Matt. She deserved praise for her handling of the situation.

Matt had tried to question Cassie, but she had stayed stubbornly silent. She did react, however, when he told her he had been due to interview her father the following day.

"Dad, my dad?" she said, looking up at him while a paramedic was putting a temporary dressing on the wound to her shoulder. For the first time she seemed a little vulnerable. "I want to see him," she said.

"Did you know he was in London?" Matt asked.

"Of course, I did. You must tell him to come here. He must come and get me out of this… this…"

Matt's only response to this was to tell her he would get someone to contact her father, that was all he could do.

He went into the hallway and got through to the chief superintendent. "As you know, ma'am, I was due to interview Al Paver tomorrow. Would it be possible to have him escorted down here from London?"

"Of course," she said, "leave it with me."

Yet again Matt thought what a refreshing change Erica Talbot was.

The ambulance took Cassie off to the hospital for further treatment, taking Tom Watkins with them in spite of strong protests from Cassie. Matt had told her he would be coming to interview her in the morning and that Tom Watkins would be standing guard outside her hospital room. This had produced a scornful scowl but no more.

Everyone was feeling relieved that the stand-off had ended without further injury. The AFOs had been stood down and two of them had already left, along with Paige Roberts, the crisis negotiator. Floyd Amory and Rhian Seddon had stayed behind to settle things with Matt and Dilys.

Matt had sent Fabia a text telling her that all was well, and he'd be home in an hour or so. He was standing talking to Floyd, when his mobile rang. He glanced at the screen, saw that it was Cath and wondered why she was phoning, then his heart sank. Hadn't Fabia told him Cath had come round to keep her company?

He pressed the green disc and said, "Cath? What's up?" His eyes widened and he said, "How long ago?"

Seeing the expression on his face, Dilys held up a hand for quiet around them. "Hang on, people, shush," she said.

"I'm still out at the house. Can I speak to her? ... Shit, shit, shit. Right, okay. Give her my love, tell her I'll be there as soon as I possibly can."

"What's up, sir?" Dilys asked. "Is it Fabia?"

"Yes. She's gone into labour. Cath Temple has taken her to the hospital."

"Well, you must go," Dilys said decisively.

"But I can't. There's still far too much to clear up here."

Dave Parry, a father of three, came over from where he'd been talking quietly to Rhian Seddon. "You should go, sir. We can finish up here."

"And we're not taking no for an answer, Matt," Dilys said. It wasn't often she used his name. "Reuben can drive you and I suggest you blue-light it all the way. Fabia needs you."

"I can drive myself," Matt said, frowning at her but he didn't say he wouldn't go.

"No, sir," Dave Parry said. "Take it from me, you won't have your mind on the driving and the last thing you need is an RTA."

Floyd Amory joined in. "Go on, get going."

Matt looked around at them all, felt a lump rising in his throat, croaked out "Thanks," and he and Reuben left the house at a run.

In spite of the siren and the flashing blue light, it seemed to Matt that the journey took an age. Reuben didn't say much, and Matt was glad of it.

When they were nearly there Reuben said, "I think the main reception will be closed by now, sir. I'll drop you off at A&E, I'm sure you'll be able to make your way to the maternity unit from there."

"Thank you, Reuben, good idea. I'm glad your brain's in gear, mine certainly isn't."

"Hardly surprising, sir. And I have a hyperactive three-year-old, my wife and I seem to spend a lot of time at A&E, I could probably drive here in my sleep!"

They finally screeched to a halt at the entrance to A&E, in amongst several ambulances. With a quick, heartfelt thank you to Reuben, who wished him good luck and all the best, Matt ran into the hospital.

Chapter 20

It was half past three on Friday morning. Matt sat in a chair by Fabia's hospital bed while she slept. He had her hand in both of his as he watched her, holding her long fingers as if he would never let them go. Suddenly he had an overwhelming feeling of déjà vu and he was back to the first case he'd tackled since he and Fabia had met up again after their long estrangement. Fabia had been beaten up and he'd been terrified that he'd lose her again, but this time permanently. The thought made him feel cold and his fingers tightened on her hand. The slight movement woke her.

"Hallo you," she said, her voice a whisper in the quiet room. "You should have gone home to get some sleep."

"I didn't want to leave you. How do you feel?"

"As if I've been beaten up," she said, unconsciously echoing his thoughts. "Where have they taken her?"

"Just to do a few tests to make sure she's fit and healthy," Matt reassured her. "Routine, they told me, when it's an early birth, and a first one for such an elderly mother."

Fabia stuck her tongue out at him, then felt down the side of the bed. "Where's that remote control thingy that lifts this end of the bed?"

Matt searched for it and gave it to her. Once she was propped up, she asked, "Can you hand me that glass of water?"

He did so and once she'd gulped down a few mouthfuls, she smiled at him and said, "We have a daughter." Her voice shook a little as she said it.

Matt grinned. "Hard to believe, isn't it?"

"I think it probably will be for quite some time," Fabia said, then, looking worried, asked, "Did they tell you how long they'd be?"

"No, but I'm sure they'll bring her back soon."

Fabia closed her eyes for a moment then opened them and looked sternly at Matt. "You really should go and get some sleep, and you'll have to have your clear-up session after last night's activities – up at Carreg Llwyd House, I mean, not here. Go on, love, I'll be fine."

It took her a little longer to persuade him but, in the end, he agreed. Dilys had arranged for his car to be left in the hospital car park and the keys had been left at reception in A&E. Matt made his way along the labyrinth of corridors from the maternity unit to reception and then to the car park. Exhaustion hit him when he got back to Morwydden Lane. He fell into bed and was asleep within seconds.

* * *

When Matt walked into the office at half past seven the following morning Dilys was already there.

"Congratulations, Matt, how are they?" Then she surprised him by giving him a hug. "What time was she born?" she asked.

"Just after one in the morning."

"That's good, you got there in time. And how's Fabia feeling this morning?"

"I spoke to her on the way in, she's fine but tired. Bethan has been given a clean bill of health after all the tests, they wanted to check her thoroughly since she's a bit premature. She's absolutely beautiful, obviously." Matt couldn't keep the grin off his face. "They're keeping them in until tomorrow, just to be sure. Look, I'll show you some photos."

He pulled out his mobile and Dilys leaned in to look. "Ah, there's a sweet little pet, and Bethan is a lovely name," Dilys said.

"Yes, it's after my sister, and her second name's Meg, after Fabia's aunt." He ran a hand through his hair. "But let's get to work. We can't spend the morning talking about my daughter – good Lord, that sounds strange."

Dilys grinned at him.

Gradually, as the rest of the crew came in, congratulations and questions about Fabia and the baby came thick and fast and the photos on Matt's phone were brought out again, but it wasn't long before Matt called everyone to order.

"Okay, people, it's already eight o'clock so we must get going. As you know, Becca has gone to relieve Tom Watkins at the hospital and we've heard that Cassie – sorry – Rose is awake but uncooperative. Sounds like par for the course. Dilys and I will be going to interview her immediately after this. Rose's father, Al Paver, is coming down from London. Would you meet him off the train, Dave? It arrives at twenty past one."

"Will do, sir, and bring him to the hospital?"

"Yes, that'd be best initially, but we'll need to interview him on his own to get some background as soon as possible. If that arrangement changes, I'll let you know."

"I've got a recent photo of him on my laptop," Dilys told Dave. "Better take that with you."

Once the whole team had their instructions, Matt and Dilys left for the hospital.

"The temptation to go and see Fabia and Bethan is almost more than I can resist," Matt said, with a glance at Dilys.

"You could after we've interviewed Rose."

"Depends how long it takes."

On arrival at the Royal Gwent they asked to speak to the doctor who was looking after Rose Spencer, as they now knew her. For Matt it seemed surreal to be back at the hospital so soon, but for such a very different reason. He told himself he must concentrate on the job and tried to push thoughts of Fabia and the baby out of his mind. He wasn't very successful.

They were led along endless corridors to a lift, went up one floor and continued down yet another corridor to a room where the doctor, a dark-haired young woman who looked as tired as Matt and Dilys felt, sat at a desk. She rose as they came in.

Matt introduced himself and Dilys, and they showed their warrant cards, then he asked, "Is the patient up to being interviewed?"

"Yes, I think so. The wound was very small. A graze, nothing more," the doctor told them. "But I'm not so happy about her mental state. Can you tell me what was behind the incident?"

Matt gave her a brief explanation of the case. Her eyes widened as he spoke, but she made no direct comment.

"I can understand your need to interview her," she said. "But she is my patient and I have a duty of care. Has she any family who could support her?"

"Yes," Matt told her. "Her father is coming down from London, he arrives later today."

"Good. That makes me feel a little happier." She got up from her chair. "If you'd follow me, I'll take you in to see her."

They made their way to a room a few doors down marked 'staff only'. The doctor tapped in a code on a keypad and they followed her in. It turned out to be a small side ward. DC Becca Pryce got up from a chair in the corner as they came in. She said quietly to Matt, "Nothing to report, sir."

On the bed, with her back turned to the door, lay Rose Paver. On her shoulder was a neat white dressing. She looked round as they came in, scowled, then turned her back again.

The doctor went around the bed to speak to her, took her pulse and then persuaded Rose to sit up and helped her to do so. "These police officers want to have a word with you, Rose."

"I don't want to talk to them," Rose muttered.

"I think it's best if you do," the doctor said, then looked across at Matt and said, "I'll send in a nurse in case there are any problems, but I'll leave you to it."

Matt walked round to take her place, followed by Dilys.

"I'm afraid you're going to have to talk to us at some point," he said. "Why not get it over with?"

She glared at him. It was a silent battle of wills.

"Do you wish to have a solicitor? Or do you wish us to contact the duty solicitor?"

"I don't need one," she snapped.

"Are you sure?" asked Matt.

Rose just nodded.

Dilys got out an iPad, tapped away for a bit then gave the date and recorded those present, and where the interview was taking place.

"We'll be recording this interview," Matt told Rose. "You do not have to say anything. But it may harm your defence if you do not mention when questioned something which you later rely on in court. Anything you do say may be given in evidence. Do you understand?"

This was received with a sneer but still she said nothing. There was a knock at the door and Becca opened it to let in a nurse. She was stocky and grey-haired and didn't look as if she'd take any nonsense from any of them.

"I'll get two more chairs," she said. When she'd done so she stood by the door, impassive, ready for anything.

* * *

Late on Saturday morning Matt fetched Fabia and Bethan from the hospital. Their occasional cleaner, Mrs Pritchard, had been in and done a thorough job on the house. The whole place looked tidier than it had in ages, and the small room above the front door that they'd decided would be a nursery, was all ready for the new arrival. Fabia had spent some time painting a mural of colourful animals on one wall, but for now the newly renovated cradle was set up in a corner of their bedroom.

That first day he kept off the subject of work, which allowed the three of them to begin to become accustomed to this enormous change in their lives, although they both knew it would take a great deal longer than just one day.

They'd arranged for Dilys to come round and meet Bethan on Sunday and it wasn't until then that they got round to bringing Fabia up to date on the case.

Dilys had arrived laden with presents and cards from Matt's team, including a soft toy red dragon from Chief Superintendent Erica Talbot. Dilys bent over the buggy where Bethan lay asleep, her tiny fists held up either side of her face.

"She is gorgeous, Fabia, such a pet," Dilys said.

"I know. I just can't believe she actually exists."

They sat down next to each other on the sofa. "There are so many cards," Fabia said. "I think we'll have to make two rows of them on the mantelpiece or start spreading them around in the kitchen. Now, you two," she went on, "while Bethan's asleep I want a comprehensive update on everything that's happened."

"This could take a while," Matt said. "I'll get some coffee."

When he got back to the sitting room Dilys and Fabia had unwrapped the rest of the parcels and were admiring the baby clothes and toys revealed.

Matt stretched himself out in an armchair and asked, "What do you want to know then?"

"All I know is that Cassie–"

"Rose," Matt corrected.

"Rose. This is so confusing. That Rose is Selina Spencer and Al Paver's daughter, as I suspected from the likeness between that photo and the adult Cassie," Fabia told them, then went off at a slight tangent. "You know what made me sure about it? It was the last time I visited Geraint. When she opened the door, she wasn't wearing her glasses and I saw the slight cast in one eye. Then Helen mentioned it, and she made the connection when I showed her the photo. I also know that she's confessed to killing Geraint, and that she had a gun and you had to get the AFOs in, but you managed to get the gun off her."

"Well, Mari did. She was incredibly brave, poor girl," Dilys said. "When her mother arrived to pick her up, she collapsed completely. Glenda Armitage was like a different person, wasn't she, sir?"

"No 'sir' needed, Dilys, and yes she was. I thought she showed a motherly side I wouldn't have expected from her."

"Nor would I," Dilys said. "A bit of a contrast to that Al Paver. When we took him in to see his daughter at the hospital, he was desperately trying to deny all responsibility for anything Rose had done. She kept saying, but you told me how much he – meaning Geraint – damaged my mother, you told me he abused her then forced her into killing herself, you said she wouldn't have committed suicide if he hadn't driven her to it."

Matt picked up the story. "He blustered a lot, but it was pretty clear she was telling the truth. He must have been drip-feeding her this poison for years."

"But how did she get the job with Geraint?" Fabia asked.

"That was a stroke of luck for her, not for Geraint though," Matt said. "She came to the UK a few years ago and worked in London, then came to Wales a year later. She was doing a pile of research on him while she was in London, although it seems she'd been collecting information about him for some time. When she arrived here, she applied for the job in the normal way, through an agency, and got it. She was making a tidy bit of money by selling off some of his smaller treasures. We've got to find out exactly what and see if we can trace them. Then she proceeded to undermine his health by feeding him barbiturates, which was why he was becoming so uncertain on his feet."

"She got them online?" Fabia suggested.

"Yup. Easy enough if you know how."

"The first time I visited him she came in with pills for him to take," Fabia said. "He obviously thought it was a normal routine, prescribed by his doctor, at least, I think so."

"Probably. We'll have to contact his doctor to find out more," Matt said.

"How did she persuade him up on to the window?" Fabia asked.

"That was a bit of luck as well," Matt told her. "She'd been going on about how much the wrought iron needed attention. I suspect she might have helped it on its way a bit. Geraint finally agreed to go up there and have a look and she just grabbed her chance. She's pretty strong, works out at the gym a lot, and she had little trouble bending and grasping his ankles and pushing him over the rail. She sounded quite proud of herself about that. But when she got back downstairs, she realised he wasn't actually dead."

Fabia's eyes filled with tears and Matt stretched out to take her hand. "This is upsetting you, my love. Do you want me to stop?"

"No, no," she said as she rubbed at her eyes with a tissue. "I want to know."

"He was pretty badly injured, but still alive, so she hit him with one of his golf clubs, just as Pat Curtis suspected, then washed it and put it back in the hall cupboard. The SOCOs have collected the whole bag of clubs and we're hoping they can find traces of blood on one of them."

"I've just thought, that rosemary Craig found in his hand, was that a sort of signature, a way of saying 'I did this' without actually confessing?"

"Yes. She actually smiled when she told us about that, as if she was pleased and wanted us to tell her how clever she was. And we found a Fair Isle jumper in her room which we think will match up with fibres found under Geraint's nails."

"Is she certifiable?"

"No, I don't think so, just completely obsessed and warped by the information – lies – her father has been feeding her all these years. He has to take an enormous amount of responsibility for what she did. I think he realised that, although he wouldn't admit it when we challenged him."

"He's such a weedy, ratty little man," Dilys said. "He reminded me of the character Timothy Spall played in the Harry Potter films."

"I know which one you mean," said Fabia. "So Gaunt and Lowe are off the hook then?"

"Not if Helen Tudor and Mari finish Geraint's biography they aren't, and they fully intend to."

Fabia grinned. "I hope they've got the letters and photographs I gave to Geraint. They could be useful."

"I'm sure they'll have access to them," Matt said.

"And what about Mari's stepfather?"

"David Singaram will go on with his investigation," Matt told her. "If we find any useful info in amongst Geraint's papers, we'll pass it on to him."

Matt paused, then said, "And there was something else in the will, something about you."

"Me?" Fabia said, eyes wide.

"Geraint had added a codicil to his will since he met you. He's left you his gold signet ring, apparently your Auntie Meg gave it to him just before he left Wales."

"Oh!" Fabia said, but she couldn't manage anything else for the tears gathering in her eyes.

The three of them sat in silence for a while until some snuffles and grunts and a high-pitched cry indicated that Bethan was awake and wanting attention. Matt went to pick her up and as he stood there, cradling his daughter, it occurred to Dilys that fatherhood suited him, he looked so comfortable holding her. She glanced across at Fabia who smiled. Dilys was sure that Fabia had just had the same thought.

Character list

Fabia Havard – artist and ex-police superintendent

Cath Temple – Vicar of St Cybi's church and close friend of Fabia

Geraint Denbigh – film director and writer

Cassie Angel – Geraint's housekeeper and carer

Mari Reynolds – Geraint's niece, co-founder and creative director of Cariad Productions

Tenniel Darling – co-founder and CEO of Cariad Productions

Craig Evans – gardener and handyman, works for both Geraint and Fabia

Glenda Armitage – Geraint's sister, Mari's mother

Jonathan Armitage – Glenda's husband, Mari's stepfather

Brandon Gaunt – a film and theatre agent

Stephen Lowe – a film director

Helen Tudor – actor and friend of Geraint's

Selina Spencer – American actress who was married to Geraint

Al Paver – Selina's husband before she married Geraint

John Meredith – local solicitor

Police personnel:

Detective Chief Inspector Matt Lambert of Newport Police – Fabia's partner

Detective Sergeant Dilys Owen

Chief Superintendent Erica Talbot

Chief Superintendent Charlie Rees-Jones, retired

Detective Sergeant Dave Parry

Detective Constable Tom Watkins

Detective Constable Sara Gupta

Detective Constable Becca Pryce

Police Constable Karim Singh

Police Constable David Hywel

Police Constable Reuben Trent

Police Constable Aidan Rogers – IT expert

Dr Pat Curtis – pathologist

Sergeant Floyd Amory – authorised firearms officer

Constable Rhian Seddon – authorised firearms officer

Paige Roberts – crisis negotiator

Acknowledgements

A few thank-yous, to Tor Amey for her advice on police procedure and the Armed Response Unit, any mistakes are mine not hers! To all my new-found friends in Hampshire who've helped me enormously with the writing of this book, you know who you are. To Ros, my boys, and Niall for their encouragement and support. And last, but not least, to Chester Felix Cat for agreeing not to sit on my keyboard and block the screen while I'm writing.

Also by Pippa McCathie:

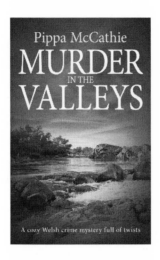

MURDER IN THE VALLEYS

The first book to feature Fabia Havard and Matt Lambert

Having left the police following a corruption investigation, ex-superintendent Fabia Havard is struggling with civilian life. When a girl is murdered in her town, she can't help trying to find the killer. Will her former colleague Matt Lambert stop her, or realize the value of his former boss to the floundering inquiry?

Available in paperback, audio, and FREE with Kindle Unlimited.

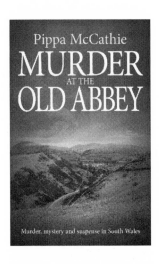

MURDER AT THE OLD ABBEY

The second book to feature Fabia Havard and Matt Lambert

When an overbearing patriarch and much begrudged ex-army officer is found dead in his home, there is no shortage of suspects. DCI Matt Lambert investigates, but struggles with a lack of evidence. He'll have to rely on his former boss, ex-detective Fabia Havard, to help him. But will their fractious relationship get in the way of solving the case?

Available in paperback, audio, and FREE with Kindle Unlimited.

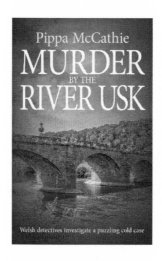

MURDER BY THE RIVER USK

The third book to feature Fabia Havard and Matt Lambert

Almost ten years after he went missing, a student's body is found. Forensics show that he was murdered and a cold case is reopened. But when detectives begin to investigate his background, many people he knew are found to be keeping a secret of sorts. Faced with subterfuge and deceit, rooting out the true killer will take all their detective skills.

Available in paperback, audio, and FREE with Kindle Unlimited.

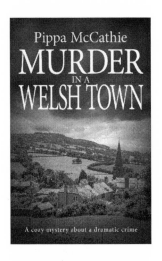

MURDER IN A WELSH TOWN

The fourth book to feature Fabia Havard and Matt Lambert

Hopes for a town pantomime are dashed when a
participant is found murdered. The victim was the town
gossip and there is no shortage of people who had a
grudge to bear against him. Detective Matt Lambert leads
the investigation but draws on the help of his girlfriend,
ex-police officer Fabia Havard. Can they solve the crime
together?

Available in paperback, audio, and FREE with Kindle Unlimited.

LIBERATION DAY

A standalone romantic thriller

Having become stranded in the English Channel after
commandeering her cheating boyfriend's boat, Caro is
rescued by a handsome stranger. But when the boat is
impounded on suspicion of smuggling, she once again
finds herself in deep water.

Available in paperback and FREE with Kindle Unlimited.

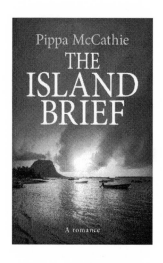

THE ISLAND BRIEF

A stirring romantic suspense

When Abi receives a surprise letter about an inheritance, it brings memories of her childhood on the island of Mauritius flooding back. Plus, a recollection of the sender, Raj, now a lawyer but then a small boy who was on the receiving end of her childish pranks. She feels the desire to return, but is it just the island drawing her back?

Available in paperback and FREE with Kindle Unlimited.

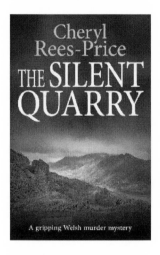

NO REFUGE by Nicola Clifford

Reporter Stacey Logan has little to worry about other than the town flower festival when a man is shot dead. When she believes the police have got the wrong man, she does some snooping of her own. But will her desire for a scoop lead her to a place where there is no refuge?

Available in paperback and FREE with Kindle Unlimited.